Trouble in a Big Box

A Kelly O'Connell Mystery

Judy Alter

Turquoise Morning, LLC
P.O. Box 43958
Louisville, KY 40253-0958

Trouble in a Big Box
Digital ISBN: 9781622370337
Trade Paperback ISBN: 9781622370320

Cover Art Design by KJ Jacobs
Editor, Ayla O'Donovan

Digital Release, August 2012
Trade Paperback Release, November, 2012

Dedication—

For Christian, who taught me about real estate and title searches and whose namesake plays a part in this book. And with thanks to Jay Mitiguy who helped me with the title of this book, and to Genie Knox who helped me with the parts about hip injuries. I'm sorry she learned that the hard way.

Praise for Judy Alter

"What a great read that I could not put down. The author had me quickly turning the pages in this suspenseful who-dun-it and the many twists and turns kept the plot moving towards a rewarding conclusion."
~ Dru Ann L. Love, on *Skeleton in a Dead Space*

"An endearing sleuth, a skeleton behind the spice cupboard, and a fistful of subplots that will keep you guessing. A nicely done debut by an author to watch."
~ Susan Wittig Albert, author of the China Bayles mysteries

"Alter gives readers a twisty plot, excellent use of setting, and a very likable protagonist. I hope this is just the first of many novels about realtor/detective Kelly O'Connell!"
~ Livia J. Washburn, author of the *Fresh Baked Mysteries*

"From her love affair with Mike to moving her mother into what has become a dangerous neighborhood for old women to solving serial killings, the reader is rooting for Kelly to win."
~Terry Ambrose, Examiner.com

TROUBLE IN A BIG BOX

Kelly O'Connell has her hands full: her husband Mike Shandy is badly injured in an automobile accident that kills a young girl, developer Tom Lattimore wants to build a big-box grocery store called Wild Things in Kelly's beloved Fairmount neighborhood, and someone is stalking Kelly.

Tom Lattimore pressures her to support the big box, and his pressure turns to threats. Kelly activates a neighborhood coalition to fight the project and tries to find out who is stalking her and why. Mike is both powerless to stop her and physically unable to protect her and his family from Lattimore's threats or the stalker. After their house is smoke-bombed and Kelly survives an amateur attack on her life, she comes close to an unwanted trip to Mexico from which she might never return.

Chapter One

I remember September 2, 2010 clearly. Mike called about eleven and asked if I wanted to meet him for lunch. For him, it would be breakfast. Mike is a patrol police officer—I've learned not to use the word "cop"—and works the late afternoon and evening shift, so he usually gets up around ten in the morning. We agreed to meet at eleven-thirty at the Old Neighborhood Grill, before it got crowded. When I got there, Mike had already secured a booth and ordered two soft-scrambled eggs with cheese and sides of bacon and hash browns. At the walk-up counter I ordered meatloaf, black-eyed peas, and green beans. We talked about the girls and their school activities. Maggie was really showing promise in ballet, which Mike said would make her walk funny the rest of her life, and Em was taking great pride in her artwork, which was probably above average for second grade, not that that's saying much. And we talked about how our beloved Fairmount neighborhood was getting back to normal after being held hostage by fear of a serial killer who targeted older ladies. Real estate was more active again, and when he was on patrol as the neighborhood police officer, Mike wasn't stopped in the streets any more by frightened women of all ages. We neither one mentioned that my mom and I came close to being the final victims of Ralph Hoskins. There was no need to talk about it—"Ralphie" was now permanently held at a facility for the criminally insane.

Mostly, we were happy. We were newly married, young—at least young in heart, since we were both soon headed out of our thirties. But we had become a family with my two daughters, Maggie now ten, and Em, now seven. We were in love, and we were happier than two people have a right to be. Maybe I should have recognized that, but neither of us had any way of knowing that Mike was about to be fighting first for his life and then his mobility, I would be stalked by a vengeful enemy, and a big-box store would threaten our idyllic Fairmount neighborhood. No, for the time, all was peaceful, and I assumed it would stay that way. Foolish optimism on my part. It's not just being married to a police officer that gets me into trouble. It's me.

After lunch, we parted—me to go back to my office, O'Connell and Spencer Real Estate, and Mike to get ready for his patrol. He kissed me on the nose and turned toward his car. I simply stood and watched him walk away, thinking what a lucky female I was. I will always remember the way he walked that day, because it would be almost a year before I saw him walk unassisted again, and he never again walked with the same casual self-confidence.

****

I'm Kelly O'Connell, sole owner of O'Connell and Spencer Real Estate. We renovate and sell Craftsman homes in the Fairmount neighborhood in Fort Worth, Texas. Mike says I have a talent for getting into trouble, but I just can't sit by and watch bad things or people threaten my children and my neighborhood. Before my "Ralphie" adventure I survived a pretty serious attempt on my life as I tried to unravel the mystery of a skeleton in a dead space in an old house. Mike Shandy, neighborhood police officer, became my protector, always ordering me to keep my nose out of police business, and during the Ralphie troubles he went from protector to companion to husband. But he still

orders me to stay away from trouble and let him handle it.
****

After that long lunch with Mike, I went back to the
office to be greeted by my assistant, Keisha, who raised an
eyebrow at me, glanced ostentatiously at her watch, and,
turning back to her computer, said, "You were gone so
long I thought you decided to do more than eat lunch."

I knew what she meant but I said airily, "Oh, you mean
run errands?"

"It don't matter to me. You just go on and do
whatever you want. I can run this office hands tied behind
my back."

"How many houses did you sell?" I asked.

"Two, and bought one. You'll find the paperwork on
your desk."

Of course, the paperwork said to call Anthony and had
the names and numbers of two potential clients. I returned
those calls first. One woman sounded like she was
seventeen but said she and her husband were new to Fort
Worth, and he was a resident at one of the hospitals. She
was a nurse. They wanted to live in Fairmount because it
was close to the hospital district, and they wanted a modest
cottage with potential. I thought immediately of Mrs.
Glenn's house, the one Anthony was working on.

Mrs. Glenn had been attacked by the serial killer but
survived. Her children, however, had sold me the house—
after Anthony convinced me it had potential—and we were
almost finished remodeling it.

The second woman wanted an already remodeled
house, in a good area—Fairmount was a good area, but it
had no single "better" area—with at least 5,000 square feet.
She was shopping in the wrong neighborhood, though I
could show her houses in nearby Ryan Place. I asked
Keisha to call her back and explain that gently.

"Sure, I'll do your dirty work." She grinned wickedly at

me. Our roles were getting reversed here. Keisha was inclined to take charge in small matters, and most of the time I welcomed that because it freed me for PR work, getting out into the neighborhood, all the things I needed to do. A large but young black woman, not fat, but big all over, Keisha dressed flamboyantly in muumuus and bright squaw skirts, both out of style on anyone but her. She came to me from the vocational program of the school district, and I blessed the day I hired her. Keisha made coffee, kept the office running, and kept me grounded a lot of the time.

****

The call came about six that night, as I was cooking dinner for the girls.

Buck Conroy, now Mike's supervisor at the police substation, minced no words: "Kelly? Get to the JPS ER right away. Mike's been in a serious accident. I'll meet you."

My hand froze on the phone—JPS was John Peter Smith, the county hospital and the closest hospital with a good trauma unit. I was speechless but Buck didn't wait for an answer. As he hung up, I went from numb with paralyzing fear to a brain that whirled with questions, the most immediate being what would I do with the girls? Mom? No, she'd worry so much she'd scare them to death. Keisha? Yes, that was it. She'd moved out of Mom's house, once the serial killer business was solved, and rented a small apartment in a larger house in Fairmount, not six blocks from my house. I called and didn't have to say more than, "Keisha, I need you right now."

"On my way," she said.

When she got to the house, I spilled out the story through tears, with two horrified young girls clinging to me. I simply hadn't been able to hide it from them.

"Go," she said. "I smell supper, and I'll finish it. The girls and I will be fine. You let us know soon as you know something."

As I left, I heard her say, "Now, girls, I don't know no more than you do. So don't start pestering me with questions. We're gonna get on our knees and pray to the Lord for Mike."

Keisha's finely tuned sense of what was right in the world came through again, and as I slammed my car door I sent up a quick prayer—a plea for Mike's survival and thanks for Keisha.

JPS was almost in my Fairmount neighborhood, so I was there within minutes. A police car waited at the ER, and one of the officers jumped out to take my car for me. Buck Conroy, Mike's colleague and often my nemesis, greeted me with his usual bluntness, "What took you so long?"

"I had to get someone to stay with the girls," I said frostily.

"Yeah, I guess they don't belong here, not now."

I wanted to scream, "Tell me about Mike! Stop talking about the girls!" Afterward I heard I said those very words in a controlled tone of voice.

"Motor vehicle accident," he said, dragging me by one arm. "Collision at an intersection. Mike was chasing a speeder, but he followed all the rules, was careful. Other car, going like a NASCAR contender, came out of nowhere and ran a stop sign."

"What happened to the driver?"

Conroy shrugged. "Would you believe he left the scene before the patrol cars got there? We know who he is—small-time crook, calls himself Sonny Adams, and we're on his trail. But his passenger, a Hispanic girl, maybe nineteen if you're generous, was dead at the scene. Thrown out of the car. No seat belt."

Someone had died! My voice quivered as I asked, "Mike?"

"Serious. They're prepping him for surgery, and they

need you to sign permission papers. He's too medicated."

Permission papers be damned! "Can I see him?"

He gave me a long look. "You sure you want to?" Then he said, "Yeah, knowing you, you do. Come on, but don't faint. Hold on to me if you need to."

I wished my heart would stop beating like a trip hammer. And why did my knees seem to be made of Jell-O?

Conroy dragged me by an officer standing guard, muttering "wife," and into a cubicle in the busy ER section. Mike lay on a gurney, his body covered to the neck with a sheet. His face was scratched and bruised and frighteningly pale, and something looked strange about the way one of his legs was on the gurney. One arm was tucked under the sheet but the other lay on top of it, and I reached for it. He had tubes in his nose and an IV ran into his arm. All I saw when I looked at him was a mess of tubes and tapes.

"Careful," Conroy whispered, pulling my hand back as I reached for him. "He's got a broken arm, other one."

"Then I can hold this one," I said, defiance creeping into my voice. "Can you leave us alone for a minute?"

My request clearly startled him, but he managed, "Uh, yeah. One minute. I'll go get the doctor. He can talk to you, and he has the papers for you to sign." And he backed out of the cubicle.

I reached for that exposed hand as gently as I could, giving it just the slightest squeeze. And I began to talk in a soft voice, telling Mike how much I loved him, how much he had to live for, how much the girls loved him.

My face was as close to his as I could get it, clinging tight to the feel and smell of him, when the doctor pushed aside the cubicle curtain and coughed gently. I straightened up, dabbing at the tears that kept creeping out of my eyes no matter how hard I tried to hold them back.

"Mrs. Shandy? Can we talk outside?"

"It's Kelly O'Connell. I kept my maiden name."

"Uh, Ms. O'Connell then," and he gestured me past the police officer. Once we were out of earshot, he said, "Sedated patients often hear what's being said, so I wanted to talk away from your husband. Let's go find a couple of chairs."

I found myself sitting at a long conference table in an empty doctors' lounge, trying to warm my shaking hands around a cup of very bad and very stale coffee. For a moment, a nervous giggle threatened to erupt because I thought of what Mike would say about the coffee. I straightened and looked at the doctor.

"Dr. McAdams," he said, holding out a hand. "I'll be operating on your husband as soon as you sign these papers. But I don't want you to sign them blindly."

Was he saying I could refuse surgery? Would Mike die if I did? I reached for the papers. "Tell me," I said and managed to keep my voice steady.

"He has a concussion, and we'll monitor for swelling of the brain. If that happens, we'll have to intervene to release the pressure. His left arm is broken, but it's a clean, simple break. We're most worried about a compound fracture of the femur at the head of his left leg—that's the bone between the knee and the hip, and his is fractured right where it goes into the hip. It's a serious fracture. We'll have to use screws and maybe plates to fix it, and he faces a long rehab process. We'll set the broken arm after the swelling goes down, not during this surgery. The rest of his injuries are fairly superficial. He was lucky."

I tried to take it all in, but it was a lot to comprehend. And all of it frightening. I knew the doctor was simplifying to the point I wanted to tell him with some indignation that I was educated and could understand a few things. In spite of that, I liked this man and trusted Mike in his hands.

"Will he walk again?"

"Probably. If he's determined and does the physical therapy." He looked at me a long moment. "His injuries are not fatal. It's a question of whether or not he'll be handicapped the rest of his life."

I knew then and there that Mike would come out of this. I would not allow him to be handicapped in any way. If he'd thought I could be a nag before, he hadn't seen anything yet. But I also knew Mike himself would be determined to walk normally again.

"Do you have a pen and can you show me where to sign?"

"Read it first," he said as he handed me the pen out of his coat pocket.

****

Thus began the longest six hours of my life. I sat in the surgical waiting room, surrounded by more of the police department than I wished and hovered over by a solicitous Buck Conroy. I called Keisha and told her what I knew, asked her to make it gentle for the girls, and to call Mom. And Claire Guthrie who had become so closely a part of our lives. But really I wanted to be alone. I wanted my own thoughts. I wanted to think about Mike and what we had together, and if I ever believed in telepathy, I wanted to send him messages about strength and hanging in there and coming home to me and the girls. And though I was long out of practice, I wanted to pray.

But Mike's colleagues crowded around me, some giving me hugs, others voicing their regret and their contempt for the kid who'd caused this and run away. They never voiced a bit of sympathy for the young woman who lost her life. Buck would have justified that because she shouldn't have been with a petty crook. Some of the officers were almost embarrassed, muttering "Sorry" under their breath and squeezing my hand. People pressed black coffee on me when I longed for a cold glass of wine.

And suddenly, there was Claire—Claire, who'd been my "help a needy neighbor" project, Claire who'd shot her husband in the rear (and some still thought later killed him), Claire who had been through the wringer. She gave me a hug without words, then pulled a chair next to mine, waved away all the officers and onlookers, and pulled one of those tiny bottles of chardonnay, what I call "travel wine," out of her bag and gave it to me with one command, "Drink this."

I drank it too fast, feeling only a slight bit of relief. My legs still felt as if they wouldn't carry me across the room, and I still leaked tears, wiping them away almost unconsciously. Claire told me that Keisha and the girls were fine, my mom had gone to my house to be with them, and they were all waiting for word. Then she took my hand, held it, and said, "Don't talk. Think about whatever you need to." Claire Guthrie, whom I once thought of as the lady with a gun, had turned into an angel. She kept people away from me.

My mind drifted back to our wedding. Mike and I had married last April, after the traumatic winter events in which Ralphie nearly killed my mom and me. We thought it was time to seize the day or whatever *carpe diem* means. Although Mom attended the local Methodist church and lobbied for a wedding there, we would not agree. We had gone to too many funerals there in the past year. I didn't exactly want a courthouse wedding, and we didn't plan to invite many people—Keisha, Anthony, his two sons, and his daughter Theresa with her husband, Joe, Claire and her two daughters. Mike's parents were both gone, and he was an only child. He insisted he wasn't close enough to any aunts, uncles or cousins to invite them, but at his suggestion, I reluctantly included Buck Conroy, the detective who'd been the bane of my existence, and his significant other, my former—well maybe still—girlfriend, Joanie. They'd bring McKenzie, her baby.

I'd met the young minister at the Methodist church during the serial killer chase and liked him, so Mike and I decided to ask if he'd perform a simple ceremony in our living room. He agreed, and we assembled everyone on a Sunday afternoon. The girls stood by us in front of the minister, and he inserted special vows for them—we became a family. After the ten-minute ceremony, Mike and I cut a Black Forest cake from Swiss Pastry Shop. Both of us love that cake and don't care much for traditional cakes. There was much toasting with champagne—over Mike's slight frown of disapproval, the girls each got a small sip in a flute. Joe took pictures, a detail I'd not thought of. It was simple but joyous, and in no time we had changed out of wedding clothes and were grilling hamburgers for everyone. Mom still fretted that it wasn't a church ceremony, and Keisha came close to pouting because there was no music. I didn't care. Mike and I were married.

Mom also fretted because I didn't take Mike's name. It wasn't proper, she insisted, and when I retorted I hadn't taken the name of my previous husband either, she replied with, "And look how *that* worked out!" Remembering the moment, I grinned just a bit, and Claire watched me carefully. Those memories made me happy.

A young doctor came through the swinging doors and asked, "Ms. O'Connell?" He was kind, polite, and, I decided, about twenty-four at the most. "Dr. McAdams wanted me to report to you." He said that Mike's vital signs remained strong, and the surgery was going well. I thanked him, but it wasn't a hearty thank-you. I was fixed on whether or not he would walk. Walk the neighborhood again, chase a ball with the girls and Gus, our dog. And, yeah, make love to me.

I looked at the clock. They were three hours into the surgery. "Claire, would you call Keisha and give them all the report?"

She nodded and then handed me the second small bottle of wine. "This is all," she said. "I figured I don't want to deal with you sloshed."

I managed a slight grin and drank it gratefully. She dialed our house, and of course Mom insisted on talking and it was some time before Claire got through to Keisha, but while her talk to Mom was reassuring, her answers to Keisha were direct. I suggested she call Anthony and gave her my phone with his number. I could hear him saying, "Mother of God!" and picture him running his hands through his hair. Another slight grin.

Dr. McAdams didn't come out of surgery for another three hours, time that dragged by. When he did push through the swinging door, his mask down from his face, his eyes were weary. Wordlessly, he sat down next to me and took my hand. Claire tactfully moved away. "The surgery went well. He's strong and in good shape, and he should walk again."

"Run?" I asked.

"That's up to him."

I asked about swelling in the brain and he replied that it seemed to be under control. They didn't foresee surgery. Mike would be dopey for at least a day when he woke up, the doctor warned.

I went in to see Mike in recovery. Of course, he was still sedated and couldn't even squeeze my hand. His color was awful, and he looked cold—and felt cold. I almost wanted to ask if they were sure he was alive. He still had breathing tubes and all sorts of stuff around his mouth and nose, so that I couldn't kiss him anywhere except on the forehead. I did and stumbled out of the area.

Conroy tried to talk to me, but Claire waved him away, took me home, and practically put me to bed. Apparently she also waved away Keisha, Mom, and the girls, each of whom was offended. She gave them a full report and said to let me sleep until I woke up. I went to sleep at seven in the morning and slept all day.

Chapter Two

I was groggy and confused when I woke up, but slowly, the real world came back to me. Mike! My hand reached for him before I remembered—the accident, the surgery. The bedroom was dark—surely it wasn't yet night. I had to get to Mike. When I stumbled into the kitchen, I found I had slept the clock around. It was after seven in the evening, dusk but not yet dark, and Mom and Keisha were cleaning up the kitchen.

Maggie rushed up to me. "We saved you some dinner. It is delish. Keisha said it's called Doris' Casserole because somebody named Doris gave her mom the recipe." It was Maggie's sweet way of telling me she was worried about me. Em came and stood beside me wordlessly for a long minute. Then she said, "I want to see Mike." Her tone implied that the statement made it a reality. She *would* see Mike.

"We've called twice," Mom said. "He's in a private room, doing fine, still groggy."

"I...I need to see him, touch him, know for myself that he's okay."

Keisha stared at me with an appraising look and sighed. "Of course you do. Go put on some sweats and we'll go."

"Sweats?" I yelled. "I have to look good for him." The second part of her sentence dawned on me more slowly. "We'll go?" I asked. "I can go alone."

"I'm going," Keisha said, her arms crossed belligerently. "You're not going to JPS alone at night. No argument. And he probably won't care what you're wearing, if he even notices."

Before I could think of an answer, the girls began to clamor to go, insisting in shrill voices that they too had to see Mike, to know that he was okay.

I gathered both girls in a hug. "No, darlings. I'll tell Mike how much you wanted to come, but you stay home. Nana will get you ready for bed…and tomorrow you can go see Mike. I promise. Before school. We'll let you be late. Your teachers will understand."

I put on a soft turtleneck and good chino slacks with a light wool jacket that I'd splurged on for fall. I wasn't going to see Mike in sweats. Maybe it was pride and maybe it was my private moment of rebellion.

No police officer jumped out to take my car this time, and we had to wind our way up several levels of the parking garage, a spooky place at eight-thirty at night. "See why I'm with you?" Keisha asked and then laughed at me. I nearly held her hand as we made our way down the dark stairwell, with me expecting someone to jump out of the shadows any minute. She was right. JPS could be a scary place.

At the door to Mike's room, I looked at Keisha. "I know," she said, "I'll just wait out here in the hall and flirt with this good-looking cop."

The policeman, tall, young—probably Keisha's age—and Hispanic, looked like he might panic, but Keisha was unfazed. "Take your time. Mr. Officer here and me are gonna get acquainted." As I entered the room, he was offering her his chair.

Mike was sort of awake, sort of asleep. When I took his hand and whispered his name, he asked, "Kelly? I thought you weren't coming till tomorrow."

"Wild horses couldn't keep me away. Neither could Keisha."

He grinned just a bit, and I kissed him—no more tubes and all that, though his face was still a mess of cuts and scratches and so was his good arm. He had a button for administering his own pain medication and wires that connected to various monitors that beeped comfortably. I asked if he was in pain, and he said not really. He was so loopy he didn't know. He began to mutter about things he needed—a Dopp kit and the like—and I promised to bring them.

Haltingly he asked, "The other car? Conroy won't talk about it."

"I don't know anything," I lied.

"Find out. Please. I've got to know. No kids? I heard this awful scream. I remember it so clearly."

Oh, Lord. Was he going to be burdened with traumatic memories—and nightmares? I shook my head, "No kids. I know that much."

He seemed relieved. Speech was an effort and words came out of his mouth so slowly that it was hard to understand him but there was obviously one more thing on his mind. "I have to get up and walk tomorrow."

"Walk!" I exploded. "You can't! You just had surgery on a badly broken leg."

"That's why I have to get up," he mumbled.

I didn't stay much longer. Mike was too groggy and clearly wanted to sleep, dozing off in the middle of one of his painful sentences.

I was loaded for bear when I left that room, sailing by Keisha and a now speechless policeman to head for the nursing station. "He says he's going to walk tomorrow," I said angrily to the first nurse I saw, "but you'll see that he doesn't, won't you?"

She didn't bat an eye. "Standard procedure. Part of therapy. The sooner they get up and walk, the better their recovery."

I was appalled. This wasn't just Mike's determination, as I'd thought, but hospital policy. "He has a head injury," I protested.

"No problem," she said and went back to her charts.

"What time of day?" I asked with as much force as I could muster. "I want to be here."

She shrugged. "Don't know, and they wouldn't let you in the room anyway."

I stalked back to Keisha and said, without a bit of grace, "Let's go."

She stood up, high-fived the police officer and said to him, "See you, José."

Once we were settled in the car—Keisha was driving because she was sure I'd be too upset to drive—I asked, "Is that guy's name really José?"

She giggled. Honest to gosh, a schoolgirl giggle. "Naw, he's Joe. Joe Thornberry, actually. His mama's Hispanic, but his daddy is Anglo. I just decided to call him José. I may be late to the office tomorrow. I'm meetin' him at the Grill for breakfast. But I'll hurry. You go on and come back here, bring the girls."

I was still marveling at Keisha, her boldness and her energy, when she slammed on the brakes. The seatbelt tightened on me as I was thrown forward. Catching my breath, I yelled, "What the heck are you doing?"

"Teaching the jerk behind me not to tailgate," she said calmly as she drove on.

But the car stayed behind us all the way home, and I could tell Keisha didn't like that. My mind was still on Mike, and I didn't pay attention. I should have.

Once we were in the house, she said quietly to me, "That car followed us all the way here and then took off like the devil was on its tail. I don't think it's a coincidence."

Usually I was the one who saw conspiracy everywhere, but now I scoffed. "Why would anyone follow us?"

Mom had fallen asleep in one of the big leather chairs,

but now she roused. "Who's following who? How's Mike?" Like me, earlier in the evening, she seemed to come from some deep, faraway world.

"It's okay, Mom. Nobody's following anyone, and Mike is okay. Kind of loopy from medication, but he'll eventually be okay." At that point, I had no idea how long eventually could be nor did I know that okay was a relative state, but I would learn. "Mom, it's time for you to go home to your own bed."

Keisha planted herself in front of me. "I'm driving Ms. Cynthia home. You can see that she gets her car in the morning when you go to the hospital. I ain't lettin' her go home alone anymore than I let you go to the hospital alone tonight." It seemed that Conroy had had someone drive my car from JPS back to the house, so we had a parking lot in our driveway—my car, Mike's car, Mom's and Keisha's. I thought it was a good idea for Keisha to drive Mom home, but Mom definitely did not agree.

She drew herself up as tall as she could, which of course didn't come anywhere near Keisha's height. "I can drive myself home."

Grabbing her keys off the table, Keisha said, "Yes, ma'am, you surely can. But you ain't going to this late at night. Kelly, I'll be back in a minute. Come on, Ms. Cynthia."

I barely had time to give Mom a goodnight peck.

By the time Keisha came back, after making sure Mom was safely locked inside with the alarm system on, I had heated myself some of Doris' casserole. It was, as Maggie said, delish—a red sauce with meat, topped by a mix of egg noodles, sour cream, cream cheese, and scallions. And then a layer of cheddar. Not good for my weight program but oh, so comforting. Before I could compliment Keisha, she said,

"Kelly, you got to be careful. I'm pretty sure that car

was following us, and now whoever it was knows where you live."

I put my hands over my ears to block out what I didn't want to hear. "No more vandalism. I couldn't take it." My old house, the one Claire now lived in, had been damaged by vandals more than once during the affair of the skeleton. Teenagers were paid to scare me away from discovering the skeleton's identity and cause of death. It almost worked, and I simply wasn't up for more.

Keisha stood waiting patiently until at last I took my hands down. "No one's going to vandalize your house, least I hope not. But we don't know why this guy followed us. Maybe I'm wrong, and it was what my momma would call a big fat coincidence. But we gotta be sure."

"You can't say anything to Mike."

She shook her head. "I ain't, and you neither. I got to go home and get some sleep so I can meet José at seven-thirty and then run your business tomorrow. You take the girls to the hospital."

"Whenever I wake up," I yawned.

As she left, Keisha turned and said over her shoulder, "It was an older Mustang. Sort of brown, banged up in a few places. Tell Conroy. No, I didn't get a plate on it."

"I'm not telling Conroy anything!"

I tiptoed in to kiss my sleeping girls and then, in my own room, stripped off my shoes, sweater and slacks and fell into bed in my underwear, more tired than I knew it was possible to be. *You haven't been up that long,* I told myself, but it made no difference. My dirty dishes were still on the table, not even rinsed or soaking.

Sleep didn't come instantly as I thought it would. Instead my mind played with an older brown Mustang, slightly battered. Who would follow me? Why? The only thing I could think of was that it had to do with Mike's accident. In spite of my bold assertion that I'd tell Conroy nothing, his words about a petty criminal driving the other car came back to haunt me. I'd have to talk to him tomorrow.

****

I woke slowly, hearing distant sounds from the kitchen.

"Maggie, do you really know how to scramble eggs?"

"Yes, I do," was the confident reply. "You get that tray and put a plate, silverware and napkin on it. Then pour a glass of orange juice." A moment of silence and then, in a frustrated tone, "I wish I knew how to make coffee."

"Yuck! Who would want it?" Em asked.

"Mom would," Maggie said. "Maybe I can make a cup of instant, but I have to hurry before the eggs get cold. Cooking is very complicated, Em."

"If you'd let me help…." Em's voice trailed off, and I envisioned a nearing squabble. I decided to lie in my bed and play possum.

What I finally got was a tray presented with love and filled with spilled, lukewarm instant coffee that tasted like dishwater, stone cold eggs, and toast with butter and jam. Maggie had thoughtfully put the salt and pepper shakers on the tray and that helped the eggs. I sat up in bed and waxed enthusiastic over this treat, then forced it all down, in spite of the fact that I didn't feel like eating at all and if I had, this wouldn't have been my choice.

"You girls are so wonderful," I said, tousling Em's hair.

"Maggie did it all," she said. "She says I'm too little to cook."

Maggie looked a bit repentant. "But I can teach you," she said, putting an arm around her sister.

"And I can let both of you cook with me more," I said. "I can see you're ready."

We bustled around and got ready for the day, although

the girls insisted on changing clothes two or three times, each time claiming they were choosing their best clothes.

"We have to look good for Mike, Mom," Em explained.

I understood the feeling.

At the hospital, they hung back a bit, clinging to my pants until Mike, now much more alert, held out his good arm and said, "Come see me, girls. I miss you."

They flocked to his side, and a long discussion about his injuries ensued. "How long will you be here?" "When can you come home?" "When can you chase Gus with me again?" "I want you to grill hamburgers." And best of all, "I'm scared when you're not there at night."

No need to remind them that a year ago he hadn't been there at night at all.

"Your mom can take care of you," he said, hugging them to him with one arm. "She will never let anything hurt you. And neither will I."

I finally pulled them away, amid protests and promises from Mike that they could come back in a day or two. We headed for school, where I would have to explain their tardiness. It wasn't every day one's stepfather—soon to be father by adoption—was nearly killed in a car accident. I thought that should excuse any tardiness. I blew a kiss to Mike and mouthed that I'd be back.

After delivering the girls to school and securing the principal's promise that this would be an excused tardiness, I ran by the office on my way to the hospital. Keisha greeted me with a black look.

"Mike's better," I said cheerfully. "Much more like himself. Not groggy."

"Good. You notice that car parked across the street?"

"Car? No." I went to the door to look out, but a sharp word from Keisha drew me back. "Could you be a little less obvious?"

I peeked through the slats of the blinds and saw a battered brown Mustang. My sharp intake of breath must have been heard in the next block—or by the guy in the Mustang. I looked again but couldn't make out much about the driver except a baseball gimme cap.

"How long has it been there?"

"Since I got to work at eight-thirty."

"You get the plate this time?"

"Nope. But you're going to when you leave out the back emergency door."

"Oh, okay." Then I switched the topic. "How was breakfast with José?"

"Dreamy. I may be takin' that man home to Mama. He's just perfect, kind of quiet. Suits me, since I'm kind of noisy."

I laughed. I'd be delighted if Keisha found a young man—as long as she kept working for me. Somehow I still wasn't taking this brown Mustang seriously. It just didn't make sense that someone would follow me. Maybe they were following Keisha? Maybe it was José's old girlfriend. After all I couldn't tell gender from the glimpse I got. "Whoever it is will get tired of staring at us. We're boring," I said. I riffled through messages, asking Keisha to return a few phone calls—to which she replied in exaggerated tones, "Yes, ma'am, yes ma'am"—and left for the hospital by the back door. When I stopped at Magnolia to check the Mustang's license plate, I saw only an empty parking place.

José had been replaced by another officer I didn't recognize, a young man with just a bit of fuzz on his upper lip where he was trying to grow a moustache.

"You can't go in there, ma'am." He blocked the door.

I moved to push him aside. "Of course I can. I'm his wife."

"No, ma'am. Doctor's orders."

Doctor's orders? Had something catastrophic happened to Mike?

My stomach lurched, and my heart skipped a beat. "What's happened?"

"They're getting him up to walk. They said absolutely no interruptions. I don't care if the president came to give him a medal, I can't let him in there. You neither." The young man was a tad nervous about his job.

"Okay, I'll wait." I began to pace the hall, back and forth in front of the door to Mike's room.

"Care to sit, ma'am?" he offered me his chair.

"Thanks." I seated myself but found I was still so restless that my right foot bounced in a crazy rhythm I didn't understand and my fingers drummed on my purse. Finally, with an awkward smile at the young officer, I got up and started pacing again.

It was hours—maybe twenty minutes—before the door opened and two women in scrubs came out, laughing of all things. "Told you so," one said.

"Well, I'm glad we were both in there," replied the other.

"Excuse me," I'm sure my voice was harsh and rude. "That's my husband. Can you tell me if he's all right?"

They looked a bit guilty, and one said gently, "He will be. He just fainted. Nothing serious."

Nothing serious! Mike Shandy never fainted in his life. Planting myself in front of the two, I demanded to know what happened.

One of the women shrugged. "We're PTs, and we came to get him on his feet. It happens all the time."

"What?" I demanded. "That people faint? Isn't that a sign you shouldn't get them up?"

"No," she said. "It's a sign that he's a macho man. We told him to wait for us to help him, but he insisted he could get up by himself. He did—and then he puked and fainted, in that order."

The second woman said, "An aide will be here in a

minute to clean him up. You might want to save him more embarrassment and wait until she's through. Besides, he's having a rough day. They'll set his arm this afternoon. Shouldn't be too bad."

Shouldn't be too bad—only because it was *his* arm and not hers they were going to set. But insisting on getting up by himself sounded like Mike Shandy, and I almost grinned in spite of myself. I went down the hall to a lounge area and began making some business calls.

About fifteen minutes later, an aide came to tell me that Mike was ready to see me. I hid my grin as I went in. "So," I said brightly, "how did standing up go?"

"Don't ask," he said glumly. "I learned lesson number one: listen to the staff."

I threw my arms around him, and this time he returned my kiss passionately. Mike was on his way to recovery.

Day followed day for the next week or so. I learned to take my cell phone and some office records to the hospital, so I could work while he was in therapy sessions, which to this point were brief but apparently intense. He came back exhausted and ready to sleep, so I sat and watched him sleep and read a book. Our days settled into a routine. I sped by to greet him after I dropped the girls at school and then spent most of the morning at the office or showing houses—or looking for a house for Anthony to renovate. He was almost through with Mrs. Glenn's house, and I scheduled an appointment to take the young nurse through it. Anthony had done wonders with what, when I first saw it, had been a dark, crowded house—old carpet, old drapes smothering the windows, a kitchen beyond repair. Now hardwood floors gleamed, the walls were a clean taupe, the windows bright with plantation shutters open for light. They could be closed at night for privacy. The kitchen was the triumph, now a small corner of efficiency. Anthony had designed it so effectively that the workflow was perfect; the appliances were top of the line. There was no room for an island, but ample workspace and a built-in cutting board made up for that. Any young couple that started their lives together in this house was bound to be blessed. I hoped whoever it was would keep up Mrs. Glenn's garden, maybe update it a bit with xeriscape plants. She had treasured her garden, though it was a bit old-fashioned with dusty miller, petunias, monkey grass, and nandinas—the latter the plant that every old lady in Fairmount had.

I spent the early afternoons with Mike. Sometimes we talked about what had happened to him. He relived the accident over and over in his mind, berating himself about what he could and should have done differently. He knew by now that a young girl had died, though I'm not sure if he knew about Sonny Adams who had left the scene. Other times, we talked about the future. He knew it would be a long time, if ever, before he was back on patrol, and he despaired about that.

"Maybe now's the time to go for that detective ranking," I said.

He waved a hand dismissively. "I'd have to pass tests and all that."

"You could do it, if you prepared."

We talked about the triathlons he wouldn't be doing—he really regretted that, and I did too. I'd been looking forward to taking the girls to races. And we talked about his work on the history of Fort Worth—that, we both knew, he could do, but it wouldn't give him the sense that he was supporting his family. And he couldn't do a whole lot at the computer with one arm in a cast, even though it was his left arm.

My late afternoons were taken up with the girls, their after-school activities, and their homework. As often as I could, I brought them to the hospital right after supper, and they inundated Mike with accounts of their daily activities.

He was happier in those moments than any other time.

Sometimes I saw the brown Mustang, but I rarely paid attention to it, and Keisha had stopped talking about it.

Chapter Three

By the time Mike had been in the hospital almost a week, he was taking halting walks in the hallway, using a walker. The only time he was in a wheelchair was when they discharged him from the hospital about two weeks after the accident and sent him to a rehab hospital.

"If we let patients use a wheelchair much, their leg muscles atrophy," Dr. McAdams explained to me. "And it's too easy to fall off crutches. A walker is a lot safer."

Predictably, Mike fumed. "Look like a damned old lady," he stormed at me.

"Why not at least an old man?" I asked but that only exasperated him more. So did the fact that a walker wasn't easy to manipulate with one arm in a cast. Mike was even told, sternly, to exercise the fingers that dangled out of his cast. And no shower while it was on—French baths for him. He really groaned at that. My offer to help was met with a withering glance, even though I meant it well—mostly.

Dr. McAdams said the purpose of the rehab was to recuperate and begin recovery therapy. What he had done in the hospital was designed just to keep him from stiffening up, not rehabilitate him. Now he'd have to learn to walk again, bit by bit, as he could put weight on his bad leg. But Mike itched to get home. He complained that he wanted to be home with us. He wasn't getting much therapy anyway—an hour a day at most. The indignity of nurses bathing him was getting to him, and he hated the food. But Dr. McAdams remained firm, and I told Mike I'd bar the door if he checked himself out against doctors' orders.

He finally laughed.

Our routine didn't change much during those two weeks. I spent early afternoons and most evenings at the rehab place instead of the hospital, but it was actually closer to my office. Yes, I would be glad to have him home, but I was so grateful that he was alive and would walk again that I easily accepted my life divided between the office, taking care of the girls, and visiting Mike.

The brown Mustang seemed to have disappeared. Even Keisha commented on that.

The young nurse and her husband, after several walk-throughs, were interested in Mrs. Glenn's house. I'd had a couple of other people look at it, so they knew they had to act quickly. They asked for a price, but Anthony had finished the house so quickly, their interest came up just as quickly, and what with my distraction with Mike, I didn't have the firm price. I'd been giving them ballpark figures. So I sat at my desk punching numbers into the adding machine when I noticed Keisha staring at me.

"What?"

"When's Mike coming home?"

"End of the week," I said. "I think I'll have a party."

"Hold on to yourself, lady. He don't need a wad of people around when he first comes home. You remember coming home from the hospital? You feel like a truck run over you and then backed up and did it again. Have dinner with the girls and save the rest of us for a few nights later."

I'd only come home from the hospital twice, each time with a new baby girl, and there were no people around because that wasn't Tim's way. I missed family—well, Mom—and friends. I wanted to show off my babies, but Tim insisted we needed time as a family and I needed to recuperate. Not that he did much for me. I cooked and took care of the girls, and he went about his business, including accepting mysterious phone calls which were, of course, from other women. Thinking about Tim made me suddenly desperate for the two weeks of rehab to be over. I wanted Mike home.

Keisha, as always, was psychic. The night before he was to come home, Mike said, "Kelly, I know how you are about celebrating with friends. But, please, could we do this quietly? Just you, me, and the girls. Maybe we can invite everyone over Sunday night. Only I won't be able to grill. Joe will have to do that."

So that's what we did. I went to Central Market for T-bone steaks—I could grill a steak myself, for Pete's sake!—baked potatoes and a Caesar salad. The classic "let's splurge" meal. One steak for Mike, and one for the girls and me to share—they were huge (and expensive). I also got a good bottle of cabernet sauvignon.

Anthony and I had prepared the house carefully. He'd built a ramp from the driveway to the front door—Mike wouldn't be able to manage even the two steps to the porch. For the immediate future, the back yard was simply off limits to Mike—too many stairs. Inside, we'd measured furniture and doorways, making sure that Mike's walker wouldn't get stuck anywhere. The girls and I went to the flower market and arranged a bouquet for the center of the dining table. We put out my best linen, silverware, and china. The sheets on the bed were crisp and clean. Everything was as perfect as I could make it. I'd even called Mom to make sure she didn't come over until tomorrow.

I haven't seen many patients come home from the hospital before, except myself, and there's a euphoria about bringing a new baby home. There was no euphoria this time, and I was unprepared for the ordeal—well, it didn't seem like an ordeal to me. Getting from the rehab facility to home wore Mike out. He was, to put it bluntly, downright crabby. Fortunately we got home about one in the afternoon, and he took a nap before the girls got home.

They were overly solicitous, hovering over him, wanting to bring pillows, water, whatever they could think of. At one point, Mike rolled his eyes at me, as if to say, "Help!" I assigned them chores, and Mike sat back to watch the news while I put the finishing touches on dinner.

It was strange having to help Mike stand from the chair to the walker, and I thought to myself that I'd develop some great muscles by the time this was over—arms and legs both. He'd learned his lesson and didn't try to brush me off. Dinner was a success. I toasted to Mike's recovery and the girls, now having learned to say, "Cheers," joined me with flutes of 7-Up. They were as delighted as I was to have him home.

Getting the girls to bed was an endless process. They whined, cajoled, and played on Mike's sympathies. He finally agreed that they could snuggle around him on the couch, and he'd read, though neither one cared what he read. Maggie read her own books these days and usually didn't like to be read to. Then there was a fuss about who got to sit on the side of his good arm—I made them both sit on the floor in front of him. No sense jostling him as they fought for the prime space. Finally I got them tucked in and began the process of helping Mike to bed.

It was indeed a process, though he tried to be as independent as possible, and I bit my tongue and stood back, letting him bump into a doorway—I won't quote what he said—and nearly fall over while brushing his teeth. At least his right arm worked, and he could do most things—but it's amazing how many things take two arms. Homecomings, I decided, were never smooth.

By the time I got him settled in bed with the latest James Patterson novel he was reading, I was so sleepy I was ready to crash. I kissed Mike hard and long, put my book on the floor, and turned out the light on my side of the bed.

It had been a big day for both of us.

"Mike? Want me to sleep on the couch? I'm afraid of hurting you in the night."

"Don't you dare," he growled.

We slept tight and close to each other, though I swear I was half awake all night, for fear of crashing into his bad leg or the cast on his arm.

****

Buck Conroy called my office the next morning. With a lot of nervousness, I'd left Mike home alone. I worried and fretted and asked him what he needed until he finally blew up and said, "I need for you to leave me alone. I'm not helpless. I can still dial the phone." He promised to keep his cell phone with him all the time.

I worried that he couldn't make it to the bathroom, get a cup of coffee, whatever. But I left, got the girls to school by the eight o'clock bell—so far we hadn't been tardy all semester except the morning we went to the hospital. I hoped we could keep that record the entire year. I was at the office by eight-thirty, knowing I'd go back at ten to take Mike to his first physical therapy appointment for a one-on-one session with a therapist.

Buck called before nine. Without a good morning or any greeting, he launched into what was on his mind: "We haven't caught Sonny Adams yet. I thought I ought to tell you, but don't tell Mike yet. He might try to do something foolish."

"I don't think he's capable of doing anything foolish right now. He can barely get from the bedroom to the bathroom. Besides, other than ticketing him for various traffic offenses, such as leaving the scene of an accident, is there a problem?"

"Yeah, there is. Word on the street is that he's talking revenge. Says Mike killed the love of his life. Of course, she just happened to be the most recent in a string of them, but he's playing it to the hilt, talking big."

"She was only nineteen, for pity's sake. How old is this character?"

"Twenty-four."

Somehow I'd envisioned forty- or fifty-something. Twenty-four made it a lot different to me.

"You noticed anything unusual at all?" Buck asked.

"Well, there was a battered brown Mustang that followed us home from JPS that first night and then kept showing up in front of the office or at the school. But I haven't seen it for a while."

"And you didn't tell me *why?*"

"Because you'd dismiss me as a nervous Nellie."

"Yeah, right. Good excuse. Kelly, we've got to keep Mike, you, and the girls safe. You can't play these games with me. I respect you...and I'll try to show it in thought, word and deed. But we've got to come to an agreement."

The very mention of the girls terrified me. "Okay. I'll keep my eyes open and tell you anything I see. Whoever that was knows where we live, where I work, where the girls go to school."

"Damn! Why are you always the one who needs a police guard?"

"You're doing it again," I said. Then, righteously, "That doesn't reflect your new attitude."

He slammed down the phone, but he'd succeeded in scaring me. Keisha came in a bit later—our office day didn't officially start until nine—and I told her about the car.

She looked serious. "Then you might want to check out that green Nova across the street."

"Are you for real? Or are you making this up?"

She shook her head. "I saw it yesterday too but didn't think it was a big deal. But if it's there two days in a row, it's a big deal."

I looked. A green Nova, again slightly battered, with the driver slunk down in the seat and wearing a gimme cap pulled low. "Wonder why whoever it is changed cars," I mused.

"Maybe the Mustang was so old it stopped running," Keisha suggested.

"Mustangs never wear out."

"So go out there and ask them why they changed cars." She was laughing at me.

Instead, I snuck out the emergency door at the back of the building and went to my car, thinking I'd eluded Sonny Adams or whoever was driving that car.

Mike was waiting at home but it took a good ten minutes to get him down the ramp, into the car, and then load his walker. He managed to move along with a kind of hopping movement so that he didn't put weight on his bad leg. It was an awkward gait, and I didn't like watching.

We were both silent, lost in our own thoughts I guess. But as I drove east along Rosedale, Mike asked, "Are you aware a green car is following us? A Nova, I think."

My heart jumped. "Why would anyone follow us?" I tried to downplay his suspicion. "I'm sure it's just someone headed the same direction as we are."

"Picked it up when we crossed Allen Street," he said calmly. "Staying a couple cars back but in the other lane to keep an eye on us. Not a really clever tail."

"Well, let's just ignore it. It probably isn't anything."

"Take a sudden right without signaling," he directed. "Then hit a right again on Magnolia."

"We'll be late for your first appointment," I warned.

"I don't care. We've got to find out what's going on."

I followed his direction, and when I turned right on Magnolia, the car sped straight ahead, apparently aware we'd detected him—or her. I wasn't ready to tell Mike about Sonny Adams yet.

"You ever see that car before?"

"No," I fibbed.

"You're hiding something from me, Kelly." His tone was level, but I knew when Mike was deadly serious.

"It was across the street from the office this morning. Keisha pointed it out." I think I added that because I needed a partner in crime.

Mike said nothing, just stared ahead, and within seconds we were at the rehab facility. "You're coming in and waiting," he said. "Then we'll make a plan."

He was not, I thought, in a good mood to begin therapy. "I planned to stay," I said. "I brought work with me." *And as soon as you're out of earshot, I'm calling Buck Conroy.* As it turned out, I never got that chance. The first session was gentle stretching, and the therapist wanted to show me routines that I could do with Mike at home. He followed every direction, sometimes doing more than he was told, at which point the therapist told him to slow down, and only do what she told him.

"Straining yourself will slow down your healing process, not hasten it," she warned.

At the end of an hour and a half, she gave us a packet of printed instructions and said she'd see us in two days.

Chapter Four

After Mike struggled into the car, he was silent until we were almost home. Then in a quiet, determined voice he said, "Green car's behind us, on our tail. Kelly, I want you to work from home now, until I can protect you."

I could see an argument ahead, and I dreaded it. This should have been the happiest time of our lives—Mike was alive, on the way to recovery. We'd come so close to losing what we had together, and we'd been lucky. Yet we were at odds with each other. Blast Sonny Adams anyway! Why couldn't the entire police department of Fort Worth catch one criminal if they knew who he was and had a history on him? And he was openly stalking one of us, mostly me.

I got Mike inside the house and seated at the dining table. He watched the noon news, while I fixed ham and cheese sandwiches. I dawdled, almost weighing the ham and cheese and spreading the mayo evenly then deciding it wasn't even and spreading it again. "Want a beer with your lunch?" I called out.

"Yeah."

Oh, good, he'll become a daytime drunk while he recuperates. Kelly, you're just looking for trouble. If he'd said no, you'd have urged him to have one and nap. Snap out of it!

I'm not sure I exactly snapped out of it. Instead I went on the defensive the minute I sat down, jumping right in: "Mike, I know you're worried, and I'm scared too—for you, for the girls but not for me. I can't figure why anyone would want to hurt me."

"To get back at me," he said, but I held up a hand.

"Wait. Let me finish first. You know darn good and

well I can't work from home. I have houses to show, houses to look at, Anthony's work to consult on. I have to be out and about in the neighborhood. I can't hide. Now given that, let's discuss what we can do to make you feel safer about all of us. For starters, an alarm system for the house?"

"I can protect my family," he growled and then looked almost surprised. "I really can't right now, can I? Okay, an alarm system is a good idea. We should have had one all along anyway. You did at the old house."

I got up for pencil and paper and made a note. "I'll take care of that this afternoon. How about if I call you, say, every two hours."

"You'll forget, and then I'll be frantic with worry. Kelly, let's ask Keisha if she'd move into the guest house. The girls would love it."

"And what good would it do? Besides, the apartment has become a workout room, with all your equipment."

"Well, I can't work out so we can store the treadmill and the stationary bike. Keisha would be another set of eyes and ears around here, and I don't know too many grown men that would want to tangle with her."

"Mike, I think she's about to fall in love and it might not be a good time for her to lose her privacy. Besides, Keisha and I see enough of each other every day. I think we'd get seriously tired of the arrangement."

"Can you take Keisha with you on your trips around the neighborhood?"

A deep sigh. "One big reason I hired her is to watch the office."

"Hire someone else."

"Can't afford it."

We went round and round. I pointed out that I have an alarm on my car. He asked me to carry a whistle, to which I agreed. He made me promise to check the back seat before I got in the car, check my surroundings, be watchful. I promised.

"One more thing, Kelly, and I insist on this: when you show an empty house, either take Anthony or Keisha with you."

That made sense. Over the years there had been incidents of real estate agents lured into vacant houses for other than real estate purposes. In fact, an agent I knew only professionally had been badly beaten in a home near Texas Christian University, the school that was an anchor for the south side of Fort Worth. I was smart enough to avoid unnecessary risk, and I knew Anthony and Keisha would agree to this.

"You know what? I'll call a staff meeting, such as it is, when I get back to the office. But I'll call first and let you know I'm there. I'll be in the office all afternoon. No running around the neighborhood today."

I kissed him, and he held me tight. "You're too precious to lose."

"You're pretty special yourself," I said, fighting to keep my tone light. "Be sure to keep your cell phone handy. Maybe we should get you one of those monitors that older people wear around their necks." Hastily, I added, "Temporarily, of course."

He started to protest, but I held up my hand again. "Fair is fair. If you fall and can't get to your cell phone, you need help. I'll look into that this afternoon too."

I kissed him again and left. I'd forgotten all about calling Buck Conroy until I looked in my rearview mirror and saw the green Nova.

Keisha greeted me with, "Conroy wants you to call him." Her eyebrows rose in astonishment when I said, "Good. I want to talk to him."

"That's a first," she muttered, turning back to her computer.

I didn't have time to say hello, before he said, "You can relax. Well, sort of. We picked up Sonny Adams, and I think we scared the daylights out of him. Petty criminal with no spine, not one of those hardened guys. He swears he hasn't been following you, and I almost believe him. Anyway, you shouldn't have any trouble from now on. He'll have to appear in court on charges of running a stop sign and leaving the scene of an accident. Doesn't seem like much punishment for the death of a girl, but he might get some time because it was a fatal accident. He made bond already."

I wondered who paid his bond because a "petty criminal" probably didn't have a lot of collateral. Conroy may have been relieved, but I wasn't. "Buck, a green Nova followed us all morning. When I took Mike for physical therapy, when we went back home, and when I came back to the office. In fact, it's parked across the street right now."

"I'm on my way. Tell me about the driver."

As I said, "Wearing a gimme cap, slumped down in the seat. Can't tell a thing about him…all morning," I heard a car door slam and an engine start.

"All morning, huh? We had Sonny until about thirty minutes ago. It's somebody else. Damn, damn, damn."

Of course, by the time he got to my office the Nova was gone. He didn't even come in, just honked as he drove by.

"Keisha, can you get Anthony to come over sometime this afternoon, so we can all meet?"

"Sure. You gonna tell me what's goin' on?"

"When Anthony gets here."

She sniffed and turned away.

****

The alarm company would install the next day—alarms on doors and windows and a separate system for the guest apartment. The monitoring company would send a man out tomorrow morning to explain the system to Mike and get it running. That was one meeting I was glad to miss.

Turned out there was another meeting I wished I could miss. Christian called from the title company. "Kelly, have you heard the rumor going around the neighborhood?"

Paranoia is so easy to come by. "About Mike?"

"No, why would there be a rumor about Mike? How is he anyway? I'm so sorry for you guys. Should have called sooner, even come by, but you know…."

"Thanks. What rumor?"

"Tom Lattimore has requested a variance to build a shopping center on Magnolia, anchored by a big-box store."

I drew in my breath sharply. "Which big-box store?"

"An upscale grocery store called Wild Things. I hear they're going to model themselves somewhat after Central Market or Whole Foods but offer more organic, more local products. Trendy in sophisticated neighborhoods like Fairmount and Berkeley. Apparently a stand-alone now, but they want this one to be a pilot project. Need a big store with lots of parking in front. They'll landscape the parking lot."

All I could manage was a feeble, "Landscaping does little to disguise a parking lot."

"Yeah, you're right. We need to work together, get the neighborhood involved to fight this. We'll have to go before the zoning commission, probably the Landmark Commission, city council, whoever."

He stumbled a bit. "Kelly, you know Tom, maybe a little better than some of the rest of us….Can you talk to him?"

Wow! That was going above and beyond. Tom Lattimore once tried to court me, and then he tried to involve me in a scheme to renovate Chase Court, a rundown but once-grand circle of houses on the edge of Fairmount. I balked, and so far Tom had made no progress on Chase Court. Maybe he'd moved all his eggs to another basket. With a suppressed giggle, I wondered if he'd broken any.

"I'll try," I said. "Over lunch." I didn't particularly like Tom. He's the kind of speculative realtor I'm not, and his schemes make me nervous, including capitalizing on the murder of several old women. I didn't want to have lunch with him—and Mike had taken an intense dislike to Tom. "Want to join us?" I asked Christian.

"Nope. I think you'll do better on your own. He knows he can't charm me. He doesn't know that about you, though I do."

"Thanks." Hmmm. Maybe breakfast, not lunch. That was it—breakfast at the Grill.

But I didn't leave well enough alone. "Christian, I know John Henry Jackson, chair of the landmark commission. I'll give him a heads up but I don't think it would be proper to invite him to our meeting."

"Sounds good." He hung up, and I began to make my phone calls.

I dialed John Henry Jackson, who always answered his phone himself. His voice boomed into my ear. "Good afternoon, little lady. What can I do for you?" He was as hearty as usual, and I guessed he'd gotten my identity from caller I.D.

"John Henry, I need to talk to you about a big-box store being proposed for Magnolia. It would violate everything the neighborhood association stands for *and* require tearing down buildings on the national registry."

"Now, Miss Kelly, don't worry your little head about that. I've heard about it, and it ain't gonna happen on my watch." I could picture him sitting in his old-fashioned office in front of his big, old roll-top desk, his tie pulled loose, his shirt sleeves stained with sweat. He would be mopping his brow with a huge handkerchief. John Henry was a big man—okay, a fat man—and he had the personal habits that went with being overweight, though he always seemed to have good hygiene.

For all his heartiness, John Henry didn't quite reassure me.

****

Anthony came about two o'clock for our "staff" meeting—the idea still made me giggle. But I laid out what was happening about the stalker and about my agreement with Mike.

Anthony was predictably angry, peering out the window and threatening, "I go get that little SOB myself and beat some sense into him." We were spared that scene because the car wasn't there, which of course set me to worrying about where it was. In front of our house? The school?

When I revealed my promise not to show a house alone, they were in fast agreement and added further threats to those from Mike if I even thought about it. Keisha sensibly suggested I see if I could get a package deal from the alarm company and secure the office as well. I made a note.

"You want me to move into the apartment?" she asked.

I looked for signs of hesitation or reluctance, but Keisha had, as usual, put her own life on the back burner. First she moved in with Mom to protect her; now she was willing to move into our apartment. I owed her more than I could ever pay in salary—or repay in kindness.

"No," I said gently. "I want you to be free to come and go with José. You worry about me during work hours and that's all. Boss's orders."

"José?" Anthony asked. "Mother of God, what have I

missed now?"

Keisha told him about José, though she was almost coy and definitely understated in the telling.

Anthony looked at me. "Miss Kelly, you approve?"

I laughed. "Yes, Anthony, I do."

That satisfied him. As he left, he shook a fist and said, "Next time you see that car, call me right away. I come. And I tell Joe about this."

****

The green Nova didn't follow me when I left the office to get the girls from school, but when I reached the school, there it was parked across the street—and empty. Usually I queue up in line with the other cars, waiting for the girls to come jump in, but this time I too parked and got out of the car to join the parents milling around in front of the school, waiting for their children. I scanned the crowd, looking for gimme caps—or, oh absurdity, men with cap lines in their hair. It's not unusual for dads to pick kids up, so there were several men but no hat lines, and only one gimme cap—on a father I knew. I was so obvious that a few friends asked me who I was looking for.

"Oh, just a new client. Not anyone you know." I couldn't exactly say "the person who's stalking my family," could I?

The girls sensed my mood too. Em, ever perceptive, said, "Mom, what are you doing out of the car, and why are you looking around like that?"

"Oh, it's just such a pleasant day I thought I'd get out and enjoy the breeze." I don't lie well.

"Something's wrong, isn't it?" Maggie asked. "Is Mike okay?"

"Mike's fine. He's waiting for you at home. Come on, let's go." I hurried them into the car which led Em to protest, "I thought you wanted to enjoy the breeze. Why are we hurrying?"

The green car was gone.

I arrived home with a bad case of the jitters, but I didn't want to tell Mike. After he returned the girls' hugs and promised to help each one with homework, he said to me, too casually, "Conroy's coming by for a beer. He wants to talk about that green Nova."

I wondered if Mike would ever learn about little ears. Maggie immediately said, "What green Nova?"

And Mike ever so calmly replied, "The one that's been following your mom."

Maggie folded her arms across her chest and stared daggers at me. "I *knew* something was wrong. I want to know all about what's going on."

"When Detective Conroy gets here, we'll all talk about it."

All my hand signals and dramatic facial expressions did no good. Mike ignored me. The girls went to their rooms to change, and I clomped about the house seething with anger. Except I wasn't sure what I was mad at—fate?

Maggie went to walk Gus around the block, as she did every day after school, though I bit my tongue to keep from warning her about talking to strangers. Maybe she should have a whistle too. I fingered the one I now wore around my neck—such a decorative piece of jewelry.

Within ten minutes, I thought she'd been gone too long and told Mike I was going to look for her.

"Kelly, she's gone this long every afternoon. Sit down and stop pacing."

"I can't."

"Well, don't make her feel like a baby by chasing her. She'll be fine. She knows the stranger rules, and there are friendly houses along her route."

A friendly house has a print of a hand in its window—a helping hand, a signal to children that people in this house will help them if they're in trouble. *Anyone could put a friendly handprint in a front window. How do you know if it's legit?* Okay, I was getting carried away here.

Maggie was breathless when she came in. "We went around the block twice and ran a lot of the way. We're both tired, and we need water." They were indeed both panting, and I got a fresh bowl of water for Gus and a glass of ice water for Maggie.

Mike sat calmly on the couch. "Remember that Dr. Seuss book, *And To Think That I Saw It on Mulberry Street?* What did you see on Alston or College? Anything remarkable?"

Maggie gave him a long look. "Well I saw that old green car, if that's what you're asking. It drove real slow alongside me, but the driver didn't say anything. That's one of the reasons we ran the last time around the block."

Mike high-fived her. "Okay, kid, you just passed the test. Good job. We're getting you a whistle to wear around your neck."

"No way. Ug-ly!"

"Your mom has one."

She looked at me and I held it away from my chest for her inspection. "We could glue jewels on it and get a fancy rope," I suggested.

I could see the wheels turning. No other girls in school wore a jeweled whistle.

But first came Buck Conroy's visit. He barged in as usual, barely said hello, and went straight to the refrigerator on the back porch to help himself to a beer. Then he plopped down in one of the big chairs and would have put his feet on the coffee table if I hadn't given him the evil eye.

"What? Mike has his foot on the table."

"Mike has a broken leg. Try it, and I'll break yours for you."

"By golly, I think she means it," he said to Mike,

planting his feet firmly on the floor. "What's gotten into Kelly?"

I hate, hate, hate to be talked about as if I'm not present or don't quite have good sense.

"I'm fed up," I said. "That's what's gotten into me. Mike was the victim in an accident, so why should the girls and I have to be so careful? It's not fair." Okay, I knew as soon as I said that, I left myself open for the classic, "Life ain't always fair" line.

But Conroy looked at me and said, "No, it's not. You get a plate on that car?"

I realized I'd had the opportunity and blew it. My chagrin telegraphed itself from my face.

"Tsk, tsk, Kelly. If you're gonna do detective work, you'll have to be better about details." He pulled a cigar out of his pocket, looked at me and said, "Just chewin' on the end, darlin', just chewin'. No way I'd dare light it in your house. Now my little wife...."

"Wife!" I exploded. "You and Joanie aren't married."

"As of last Saturday, at the courthouse, with McKenzie as our only guest. Made it official."

Of course we both offered congratulations, and Mike went on a bit too long about the bliss of the married state—was I hearing sarcasm? I offered to throw a party, an offer that Conroy declined without consulting Joanie. I was still mulling over the marriage and trying to think of Joanie as Conroy's wife rather than girlfriend—with someone like Conroy, that's a huge change in status—when Mike said dryly, "Can you two stop baiting each other long enough to discuss this situation with the green Nova? And, Kelly, would you call the girls in here?"

"Can we talk without them first?" Buck asked.

We agreed, and he launched into what he knew. It wasn't much. Sonny Adams said he knew nothing about threats. The dead girl's name was Rosalinda Garza. She was nineteen, from a poor family on the North Side. They thought she'd struck gold when Sonny took an interest in her.

"Have you talked to the family?" Mike asked.

"Yeah, they're grieving. And they're mad. I'm thinking they'd be more likely to go after Sonny and that's why he's hiding."

I filed that away in my mind—something to follow up on, without telling either Mike or Buck. They'd have fits if they thought I was investigating the Garzas on my own, but of course that's just what I intended to do.

"Have you talked to your punk friend Joe Mendez?" Conroy asked, looking directly at me.

Before I could fly off the handle, Mike said, "Buck, he's not a punk. He's really straightened his life out. Almost has an AA degree from Tarrant County College. Devoted to Theresa."

Conroy waved a dismissive hand. "I know all that, and I almost believe you. But he might know something. You can talk to him better than I can."

For sure, I thought, as I added that to my to-do list. Why hadn't I thought about it before? I itched for Buck to be gone so I could call Joe.

We finally did call the girls into the room and explained to them that someone was following all of us. We stressed that they were not to be afraid, but they *were* to be cautious.

Em ran to me and buried her face in my lap. "I'm scared, Mommy."

I stroked her hair. "Don't be scared. Mike and I won't let anything happen to you. We'll get you a whistle just like Maggie's, okay?"

She raised a tear-stained face. "Okay. I'll be brave…and cautious."

Chapter Five

The next day I went to Hobby Lobby and bought sequins and bits of jewel-tone stones, a pink cord for Em and a turquoise one for Maggie, and the glue to hold everything on to the whistles. Then I went to a hardware store for whistles. I didn't even look for the green car.

Once back at the office, I called Joe. "Hi, Joe. It's Kelly."

"I always recognize you, Miss Kelly. What's up?"

"Theresa gone to work?"

"Yeah, but I can have her call you tonight. I don't go in until two this afternoon. I'm studying."

"Well, I hate to interrupt that, but how about lunch, just you and me? The new hamburger place on University Drive?" The Grill was too crowded and noisy at lunch for a private conversation. I didn't want folks overhearing what I wanted to ask Joe.

"Miss Kelly, you're up to something again," he said. "You sure it's okay with Mr. Mike?"

I wanted to remind him I didn't have to check every move with "Mr. Mike" but I sidestepped the issue. "Well, you know he can't get around much, so I'm doing some legwork. I have to take him to therapy this morning, but how about if I meet you at noon? That'll give you plenty of time to get to work."

"Yes, ma'am. I take the bus, you know. Theresa, she's got our car."

"Bother. I'll meet you at, uh, what's close to your house? That new sushi place...."

"Can't do sushi, Miss Kelly. Just can't do it. I even

tried once."

I laughed. "Okay, the Paris Coffee Shop at noon, and then I'll drive you to work."

The Paris Coffee Shop was neither quiet nor empty at noon—people stood in line for the meringue pies. But they served a fine blue-plate lunch. Joe and I both ordered chicken-fried steak with mashed potatoes and green beans. And I ate every bit. No wonder I always had what I delicately referred to as a "weight concern."

We chatted about Theresa—they had put back enough money that she had enrolled in one class at the county college this fall, even while Joe finished the last of his work on an associate degree. "I want to go on, but I'm not sure how to do it. One of my teachers says I got a good enough GPA for a scholarship. He said I should try for Wesleyan."

Texas Wesleyan University welcomed non-traditional students, had low tuition, and a generous program of scholarships and grants. "Let's see what we can work out," I said.

He raised his hands, palms toward me. "We can't take any help from you, Miss Kelly. You already done enough. Now tell me what's really on your mind."

"A girl named Rosalinda Garza. Know her?"

"Miss Kelly! Do you know how many Garzas there are in this city? No, I don't know her. Sorry." He pushed his plate away as though that ended the conversation. "Sorry, after this good lunch, that I can't help you."

"Wait! How about Sonny Adams?"

His face darkened. "Yeah, I know him by reputation. May have met him a time or two, but he's nobody I'd mess with now. Little dude who thinks he's big time. What's the connection?"

I explained that Sonny Adams was the one who had run into Mike, and Sonny's passenger, Rosalinda, had been killed. Now Sonny was claiming she was the love of his life.

"Probably was," he mused, "at that moment. I bet he's got a new chick by now, may even be on the second or third. So why do you want to find this girl's family?"

"Someone's following me, and Sonny Adams was talking revenge, though Conroy says he thinks he scared the idea out of him. Adams faces charges of running a stop sign and leaving the scene of an accident but that's all so far."

"So what do the Garzas have to do with this? They've lost a daughter but I don't think they'd follow you. Not the way my people react. If they wanted a fight, you'd already have it."

Joe brought up a good point, one I should have thought of. "You're probably right, but I just want to talk to them."

"Miss Kelly, let Buck Conroy do it. You shouldn't be going up to those neighborhoods by yourself. Where'd she live?"

"Off Twenty-Eighth Street."

"I gotta get to work. You sure you don't mind driving me? I'm kind of late for the bus now."

"Sure."

The green car followed us from the Paris Coffee Shop parking lot to the Southwest YMCA. I didn't mention it to Joe, and as he got out he said, "You be careful. Theresa and I, we come see you soon."

"Good." As I drove away I hoped I hadn't gotten Joe in trouble. He was still on probation, and if he decided to do anything on his own—I shut my eyes to blot out the thought and almost sideswiped a car pulling out of the YMCA parking lot. *Focus, Kelly, focus on what you're doing this exact moment. Stop racing ahead in your mind.*

But racing ahead was what I was doing. Could I find the Garza address and run up there before time to get the girls? Obviously not. In fact, how was I going to find the right Garzas in the long list in the phone book? I should have asked Joe more questions. Obituaries! They'd give me a clue but I'd have to go back to the day she was killed or shortly thereafter—now about five weeks ago. It meant, I feared, a trip to the *Star-Telegram* archives.

Back at the office, Keisha took one look at me and said, "You're up to something you shouldn't be. Remember what you promised Mike? Where am I going to have to go with you?"

I considered a minute. Maybe she was right. She should go with me. "To see Rosalinda Garza's family—when I find them."

"The dead girl? You have completely taken leave of whatever sense the good Lord gave you. Do you know what Buck Conroy and Mike would say?"

"Yeah, I know, but you're not going to tell them," I said.

She crossed her arms and stared at me. "Beats me, why I keep working for you. Guess I'm as big a fool as you are."

I left to get the girls. When we got home, I spread a thick pad of newspapers on the dining table, and got out the whistles, jewels, and sequins I'd bought. The girls clustered around, and I told them they could design their own whistles but they needed to remember that the glue held instantly, so there was no gluing and then changing their minds. I'd peek at them now and then, but I didn't want to tell them how to do it.

"Mike," Maggie asked, "you want to help us?"

"I'm not much good with sequins, Maggie. You'll do better without me."

So they worked. In the end, Em's methodical mind created a whistle with stones in precise circular patterns around the round part, and careful stripes on the straight, square part of the whistle. Maggie's designe was more free form, indicative perhaps of a free spirit. I put them aside to "set" and praised both girls. After dinner, we'd thread the cords onto them, and the girls would wear them to school the next day.

"Maggie," Mike asked from his permanent position in one of the big chairs, "do you know when to use the whistles?"

"When I see that green car," she answered positively.

"Maybe not just when you see it, but if anyone gets out and approaches you or talks to you. It's particularly important you wear it when you walk Gus."

That was an argument between Mike and me. I wanted her to stop walking Gus and run with him in the backyard. Mike said I couldn't cage her up. I kept quiet, but if anything happened to her...my mind didn't want to go there.

****

Claire called late that afternoon and asked if she could come over with a bottle of wine. I checked with Mike who said he'd be delighted to see her and wouldn't she stay for supper, whatever it is. I thought that was not a vote of confidence in my cooking on Mike's part, but I relayed the message.

Claire laughed. "I have girls to feed, remember. Even if one is in college. No, I just haven't seen you all since Mike's surgery, and I'm way overdue in checking on you."

Mike and Claire didn't always see eye to eye. Mike was the officer on duty when Claire deliberately shot her husband in the derriere, and when Jim Guthrie later died in a one-car accident, Mike really suspected Claire of having put a Mickey in his drink. Furthermore Mike didn't like it that I let Claire live in my guest apartment during the divorce negotiations before Jim's death. But now it all seemed to have worked out, and I hoped they would be friends.

Claire arrived waving not only a bottle of chardonnay—which she knows I love—but a chicken pot pie casserole she'd made. "I'm sure you've got enough on your mind, Kelly, and I just thought this might be a treat."

Before I could thank her Mike said, "Thank heaven, Claire. I thought I was going to starve to death." His eyes were twinkling like the old Mike for the first time in weeks, and when I gave Claire a hug, it was extra tight with an exchange of smiles that she understood.

"Okay, Mike, how are you?" she asked bluntly.

"Like a damned old woman. Can't go anywhere without my walker. Need Kelly to help me go to the bathroom, brush my teeth, all those things of daily living that I took for granted."

"Good lesson in humility," Claire said, without a trace of pity.

"Well, I guess you're on Kelly's side," Mike complained in mock frustration.

"No," she said slowly, "I'm rooting for both of you. I just want to know what I can do to help."

"Cook," Mike said plaintively. "You know Kelly's not the best cook."

"She's getting better all the time, Mike Shandy, and don't you forget it. Haven't Cynthia and Keisha been over here cooking for you?"

"No. I think Kelly forbid them."

Well, maybe I had, and maybe it was time to rethink that. Of course I opened my mouth before I thought. "Let's have a potluck this Sunday. Claire, you and the girls bring whatever you want, and I'll get Keisha and Mom to bring things. Why, I bet I can work it so I only have to provide a frozen ice cream cake from Braum's."

"That's my girl," Mike laughed.

Claire, always attentive to the girls, exclaimed over the jeweled whistles and declared she wanted one, plus one for each of her girls.

Maggie, who had been wary of Claire for a long time,

said, "We'll make them, won't we, Em? Mom will get us some more stuff to do it with."

"No, no," Claire said. "I'll bring the materials—maybe Sunday night when we come for dinner. Hmmm…Kelly, remember the chicken casserole I made the night I moved into your garage apartment? I'll make a double batch of that."

Of course I remembered. That was the night after she "shot Jim Guthrie in his ass," as she so delicately put it. I would welcome the casserole, and the girls would welcome the attention of making whistles for Claire and her daughters.

We chatted. Claire's girls, Megan and Liz, were doing well in school and seemed to be adjusting to living at home with Claire in charge again after a disastrous period of living with their father. Claire's job as hospitality person for a small local bank was going well. The world seemed in order—except for Mike.

Neither of us said anything to her about the stalker but he or she was always lurking in the back of our minds. "You're sure everything's all right?" Claire asked, "Do I have to ask Keisha?"

She knew me too well, and she and Keisha were now allies in the "Keep Kelly Safe" club.

"Oh, a strange car has been following me, so we're being extra cautious. I don't think it's anything to worry about." I tried to signal with a nod toward the girls that we'd talk about it later, and Claire nodded that she understood, but then added, "A kind of old green Nova? I saw it parked down the street."

"That's it," Maggie said, "and I'm not walking Gus alone this evening."

Claire always rose to the occasion. "Come on, let's go walk him together. We'll walk right by that car and show that person we're not afraid."

They were gone about fifteen minutes, but I didn't fret and worry like I had before. When they came back, Claire was a bit out of breath. "Gus sets some pace," she said. "I need just a bit more wine before I drive home."

"Miss Claire says that's a young girl in the car," Maggie said, as proud as though she herself had discovered this fact.

"Pretty sure, but that's all I could tell."

Somehow I found that reassuring, though I well know women can be as deadly as men. Hadn't Jo Ellen North killed my ex-husband and come way too close for comfort to killing me?

As she turned to leave, Claire said casually, "I'm about to start private yoga lessons. Want to join me? My treat. It would be good for you. Stress release and all."

I told her I'd think about it though the idea didn't appeal to me.

After supper, I called Mom and Anthony, asking them to come to supper Sunday. Anthony said he and the boys would be there, but Mom hesitated. Mom had kept her distance since Mike had been hurt, and I thought it was out of consideration for his privacy. Keisha burst that balloon by telling me Mom went to the church almost every day, volunteering for this or that from answering the phone to helping sort donated clothes for needy children. She attended sewing circle and a senior citizens fellowship that offered daytime trips to various places. Now, she said, "That's the Sunday night fellowship supper, and I hate to miss it. But I haven't seen you much. Yes, I'll come. And I'll bring a pie."

I wanted to say sarcastically, "Don't bother if it's trouble," but I knew my hurt feelings would be showing. When Mom moved down here, I was afraid she'd be on top of us, and now I bet I hadn't seen her in over a week.

"Keisha," I asked next morning, "does Mom have a

new boyfriend?"

"Not that I know of. But don't be surprised if one turns up sooner rather than later."

I went on to tell Keisha about my planned dinner party, adding, "Bring your mother if you want."

With a sly look, she said, "I'd rather bring José. I've been seeing him now and then."

I knew Keisha well enough to know that translated into she'd been seeing a lot of him. Somehow I'd also lost track of Keisha while I concentrated on Mike and a green Nova. I really needed to pay more attention to my circle of close friends.

"Bring them both," I said.

Later, Keisha answered the phone with "O'Connell and Spencer Real Estate," then said, "Yes, she's right here. Just a minute." Then in proper professional tones but with a grin on her face, she said, "Mr. Lattimore is on line one for you."

I'd deliberately put Tom Lattimore to the back of my mind, though every once in a while he nudged to the front and I knew I should call him. Now, I answered the phone with, "Hi, Tom," and he replied too quickly, "Kelly, how are you? And that husband of yours? Sorry to hear about his accident. Those cop chases"—I could almost hear him going tsk, tsk—"always so dangerous."

"It wasn't Mike's fault. The other car ran a stop sign."

"Of course, of course. Young girl was killed wasn't she?" He wasn't getting this conversation off to a good start. "But that's not why I called. I have a big deal in the works, and I want to talk to you about it. You may want to be part of it."

In other words, he needed me to do something. "I heard about it, Tom, and I'd like to talk with you."

"Good, good. Too late to ask you to lunch today?"

"I have to take Mike to therapy at ten and then get him

home and feed him, but I could meet you by 12:30."

"How about Lili's at 12:30?"

I hesitated. Mike and I considered Lili's our special place. When we were dating, a lot of our evenings started off there and ended in Mike's bed. I hated to sully the memory.

"How about the Grill?"

"No privacy. What I want to talk about is still pretty confidential."

Not as confidential as you'd like to think. And Lili's isn't all that private.

We finally decided on Chadra again—that's where we'd met when he'd tried to come on to me. Curiosity about who Tom might be seeing now flitted through my mind, but I really didn't care. I bet he left some angry husbands in his wake—and probably their wives when he moved on.

"See you there at 12:30," I said.

I hadn't told Mike about Christian's phone call of warning, the big-box development or any of it, so I explained it on the way home from his physical therapy, ending with my lunch with Tom Lattimore. His predictable response was a muttered, "I don't like that guy."

"I don't much like him either, but this is business, not an assignation," I said.

"It better not be."

Chapter Six

After getting Mike settled and fixing him a sandwich and a beer, I was unintentionally ten minutes late getting to Chadra. For once, I didn't have to sit alone at a table waiting, looking like I'd been stood up. Tom was there.

He greeted me with a peck on the cheek and "It's been way too long, Kelly. You're looking great. Marriage must agree with you."

We sat, I ordered ice tea, declined the buffet on the grounds I ate too much last time, and ended up with a delicious bowl of tomato-basil soup and a small house salad. Tom excused himself to go to the buffet and came back with his plate loaded. I was glad I had resisted.

Tom had requested a corner table, well away from other diners. Even so, he leaned in confidentially as he spoke. "Kelly, I've got a big deal going, a shopping center on Magnolia."

"I heard, Tom. Where on Magnolia?"

"Just west of Hemphill, south side of the street. Across the street from the Paris Coffee Shop and those offices. I think we can do it with two square blocks."

"Those buildings have a historic designation. You can't touch them," I said.

"Just some junk things. There's a new sushi restaurant—I hear it's good by the way, but if so, they can relocate. Let's see, one of those yoga places, a taco place, that small independent bank that will probably get picked up soon by one of the big banks anyway. Stuff like that. I guess there's an antique or junk store. Oh, and an old guy who repairs old clocks, has a ton of them in a jumble in his shop."

Those weren't junk businesses to me. I banked at that bank because I liked having everyone from tellers to bank officers call me by name and take a real interest in my business. And now it was where Claire worked. I had sold the yoga studio property to the young single mother, who took a chance with her livelihood and her child's well-being to make a dream come true. I checked on her from time to time—she wasn't getting rich, but she was hanging on. Taking her classes was one of the things I told myself I'd do when I had time—somehow that appealed to me more than Claire's offer. Keisha sometimes brought us tacos for lunch from that taqueria. Those businesses were more than old buildings. They were people to me—and that's what matters in Fairmount.

"The businesses, junk or not, aren't the point. The buildings are on the national historic register. You can't just tear them down." At one square mile, Fairmount is the largest historic district in the Southwest.

"We can get a variance. This project is backed by big people. Gas wells. People who have power in the city. We'll build to fit the neighborhood, believe me. Nothing stark and modern. We might even get Mike Smith to move the Paris Coffee Shop to our property."

Mike Smith would love that. His second-generation family business part of a shopping center.

"What's the big-box store? I heard some kind of new grocery store."

"The Grapevine's good on this one. That's close. I'm talking with people behind a new store, Wild Things, an upscale grocery store, like a mini Whole Foods or Central Market, only more focus on local products and less on upscale and gourmet. Locavore is a big thing these days. Golden opportunity for me. They'll construct, manage, all I have to do is…." His voice dropped off.

I'd heard all that or most of it from Christian, but what was Tom's part? "All you have to do is what?" I prompted.

He looked startled. "Pardon me?"

"You said all you have to do is but you never finished the sentence."

Nervous laugh. "Oh, that. All I have to do is act as liaison with the city, help them get established, do a little marketing."

He was covering something. "Tom, you know as well as I do that this is exactly what the neighborhood doesn't want on Magnolia. We're trying to improve and restore the entire area, make it like it used to be, not add a lot of unsightly on-the-street parking lots plus all the traffic a shopping center would bring. I can't support you on this." I didn't say that if he built across the street, on the north side of Magnolia, he'd be out of Fairmount. It would still be a travesty. Besides, the spaces on the north side were taken up with new professional buildings, built within the last couple of years and designed to blend into the area. Several blocks west you got into smaller businesses—junk, Tom would have called them. Lili's Bistro, the restaurant Mike and I loved, Nonna Tata, another favorite, a Middle Eastern restaurant that pre-dated the influx of new restaurants, a Curves Studio, a Mexican restaurant that served authentic Mexican food rather than Tex-Mex and was a breakfast favorite for residents.

"You're wrong, Kelly. The young professionals who live in Berkeley and Fairmount and Mistletoe Heights will be delighted to have an upscale grocery—with a café, meals to go, all that good stuff. We've got support, petitions signed, the whole works...." He watched me for a reaction, and when he got none, he said, "I'm presenting the proposal to the zoning board next week and I'd love to have your name on it as a supporter. I'll give you leasing privileges on half the small stores if you can bring in suitable tenants."

"There's not room for satellite stores along with a big box," I protested. "You'd need at least two full square blocks." My mind said, *A huge chunk of Fairmount.*

"That's what the architect's plans are projected on."

"Why not put it on Eighth Avenue, between Fairmount and Berkeley and closer to Mistletoe Heights and Ryan Place? Those are all target neighborhoods."

"There's already Fiesta on Eighth. Not room for another big grocery."

"Even one so different?" I saw what his problem was. There was no land that would work on Eighth, and not enough adjacent small businesses to tear down and create the space.

The more he talked, the more I tuned him out. When I did speak, I almost thought someone else had taken over my voice, because I was uncharacteristically forthright and rude. "Tom, I'm going to fight you every inch of the way on this one—petitions, zoning authority, city council. You name it."

His voice was deadly calm. "Don't fight me, Kelly. It could be dangerous. I have big money behind me on this one, people who aren't afraid to use their power."

"Well, I'm not afraid to use my voice," I said. "Thanks for lunch." And I rose, leaving half a bowl of soup and an untouched salad behind me. Tom just watched me go. I wondered if he'd anticipated my reaction.

My main worry was that Tom had really gotten the jump on any opposition. To say he had support could mean anything or nothing. But if he had petitions from Fairmount residents, that was a whole different kettle of fish.

Back in the office, I called Christian and motioned Keisha to listen in. "I just had lunch with Tom Lattimore. Told him I'd fight him all the way. I think we should start with the Fort Worth League of Neighborhood Associations. But Tom's already got petitions."

"I don't need fancy expensive groceries," Keisha muttered.

I ignored her. "Christian, I called John Henry Jackson at the landmark commission and he sort of brushed it off, said not to worry. I don't know if I'm comfortable with that. John Henry doesn't have much background in preservation. He got the landmark job by asking for it."

Christian sighed. "That's part of why preservation is such an uphill battle. People get involved without knowing what they're doing."

I went on. "I'll draw up a petition, and we can get Jim Price to check it from a legal perspective. Nice to have a lawyer as current president of the Fairmount Neighborhood Association. We should meet quickly."

"Good idea. The commission has a strong voice at city hall, and they're really an advocate for preserving older neighborhoods."

"Jim Price can call a special meeting of the neighborhood association."

"Slow down, Kelly. We may have to wait till Lattimore makes a specific proposal before we can counter with petitions."

"He says he's presenting it next week. Wanted to have my name on it as a supporter."

"Interesting. Once he presents it, his proposal becomes a public document. I think it would be really important to see who he's in bed with. I doubt there are many if any names from the neighborhood. I think I'll have breakfast at the Paris Coffee Shop tomorrow and talk to Jim."

"Christian, one more thing. His last word to me sounded like a threat. Said he had big money behind him and people who weren't afraid to use their power. I didn't ask what kind of power, but he mentioned oil and gas money. Be careful."

"Oil and gas money is all over Texas, let alone the county, these days. But I'll be careful. I'll talk to you tomorrow, and we can compare notes."

When we hung up, Keisha looked at me and said, "You got yourself into the middle of it again, Kelly. Mike is *not* going to be pleased."

I was wondering if people with money and power hired young girls in green Novas and brown Mustangs.

****

Thursday afternoon I checked the obituaries, but the *Star-Telegram* didn't keep four-week-old ones online unless the person was a really major figure. Trying to avoid another long day lost in the archives of the paper, which are in the University of Texas at Arlington library and meant a good thirty-minute trip each way, I called Martha Blackmon, a features writer I knew casually who had helped me once before. When I outlined my request, she laughed and said, "You do come up with the strangest requests, Kelly. Sure, I'll see what I can find and email you. Give me your email again."

Good as her word, she was back to me with some information before I left to get the girls. Rosalinda Garza was the daughter of a single mother, Lola Garza. A quick look at the phone book showed only one Lola Garza on the near North Side. I resolved to pay a sympathy call the next day and thought that maybe a Ranch Oak spiral cut ham would make a good gift. I admitted to myself that over a month later was a bit late for a sympathy call, not to mention the traditional gift of food. But I guess I was imagining that Mrs. Garza could use a little extra food. Martha's email indicated that Rosalinda had three brothers and a twin sister. The latter bit of information gave me a real stab in the heart.

I ordered the ham, to be picked up the next morning at nine, and went to get the girls, admittedly feeling a bit righteous. No, I did not tell Keisha, Buck Conroy, or Mike what I was planning to do. Sometimes I'm a bit slow to learn life's lessons.

For once, Mike didn't ask, "What are you hiding from me?" He and the girls seemed completely oblivious to the fact that I had a secret plan, although I usually wore such plans plastered on my face like a poster shouting, "Ask me what I'm about to do."

We had a peaceful evening—I grilled hamburgers that Mike said were almost as good as his, the girls did their homework without protest, and when they were settled in bed with their books and a fifteen-minute warning, I helped Mike with his stretching exercises. He was frustrated—and a bit grouchy—because he wasn't making progress as fast as he wanted. I pointed out it was only five weeks, and he was beginning to bear a little weight on that leg. He refused to take walks, although they were recommended, because he wasn't going to be seen in "his" neighborhood on a walker. Pointing out that he was a non-cooperative patient didn't help. Lately at therapy sessions they'd been keeping him longer to make him walk the track, which he could do with his walker and about half his weight on his bad leg. I suggested he ride the stationary bike in the garage, but he pointed out that he hadn't been okayed to use it yet.

"Well, ask about the bike. You could go out the front door to the apartment. See, isn't it a good thing Keisha didn't move in there?"

He gave me a dark look, and I subsided. Mike, I had discovered, was not an easy patient. Men never are, but somehow I expected more of him, too much probably since he was almost always good-natured and easygoing. Only a few things could push his buttons, but being handicapped was one of them. He itched to get back to work, even if it was a desk job. "I'd answer the damn phones," he exploded.

The next morning I kissed him goodbye and told him I'd see him at noon, even suggested we go to the Grill for a change. It wasn't a therapy day, so I had the morning free. I walked the girls into their classrooms and hugged them goodbye—Em would still kiss me, but Maggie was beyond that—and left for the North Side with a light heart.

Keisha was the only fly in my ointment. When I ran by the office, she asked, "You're going to be out of the office *why?*"

"I'm going to pay a sympathy call on Rosalinda Garza's family. But don't tell Mike."

"The minute you say don't tell Mike, my radar goes into overdrive. Just what do you think you'll accomplish?"

"I want to find out who's stalking us."

"And you think one of them is going to come right out and say, 'Yeah, I been following you'?"

I didn't know what I expected but I didn't tell Keisha that. Just told her to be sure to watch for calls from Christian or Tom Lattimore, and I'd be back before lunch.

"Don't you bother yourself about this office. I can sell real estate. But I thought I was supposed to go with you on this jaunt."

"I decided I can do it alone. You stay here and sell real estate."

Hmmm. Maybe Keisha should get a license. What a great idea to explore—but not now.

The Garzas lived in a small clapboard house, once painted white but now faded to a dingy gray where the paint hadn't completely peeled away. The front yard was surrounded by hurricane fencing, covered by struggling ivy that could soften its lines if it ever grew lush. There was monkey grass along the walk to the porch, and I could see where summer plants, now withered, had been. A bent mini-blind covered one of the front windows. The whole picture was of a home where someone tried desperately to keep it up but was losing the battle.

I knocked and a teenage boy, probably fifteen, opened the door and demanded, "Yeah?"

Why isn't he in school? "Is your mother at home?"

"Yeah. I'll get her." And the ill-mannered child (not the first word that came into my mind) closed the door in my face.

In a few minutes that seemed like forever, a worn-looking woman probably in her forties but looking older came to the door, wiping her hands on her apron. "Yes?" There was neither warmth nor hostility in the question—and very little curiosity.

"Mrs. Garza, my name is Kelly O'Connell. I'm married to the police office whose car Sonny Adams hit the night your daughter died." Now there was a blunt opening.

She started to close the door, but I put my foot in it. "I came to tell you how terribly sorry I am about your loss."

"Why should you be sorry? Your husband is alive, isn't he? That's what they told me."

"Yes." I drew a deep breath. "He was badly injured, but he's alive. That doesn't make the loss of your daughter any easier. May I come in?"

She stepped aside and motioned me into a darkened room where the TV blared and teenagers lounged on a sagging couch. Only the girl, who I guessed to be Rosalinda's twin, looked up at me. None of them greeted me, and their mother did nothing about introducing me.

"I…I thought you might like this ham. I wanted to do something to express my grief."

The young girl stood suddenly and stepped belligerently toward me. "Take your damn ham. There's nothing you can do. Your husband killed my sister."

I looked at her, all bravado with a bandana tied at the

back over her hair, too much make-up, a tight shirt that didn't quite reach the top of her equally tight jeans—and she had a ring in her belly button. I only glanced and then resolved to look elsewhere. In fact, I looked her straight in the eyes. The longer I did, the more anxious she became, darting her eyes away, then looking to see if I was still looking. That old dominance trick. What I thought—hoped?—I saw was a scared girl, hiding under bravado. If her sister died, could it happen to her?

This wasn't the time to argue that she should direct her anger at Sonny Adams, or at least I didn't think so. "My husband is devastated by what happened."

"Sorry won't cut it," she said, while her brothers looked on with more interest now—the first sign of life I'd seen in these apathetic kids, all of whom should have been in school.

"Bella," Mrs. Garza pleaded, "the lady came out of kindness."

"Kindness my ass. She's got a guilty conscience. I will have my revenge someday." She turned away, but I heard her mutter, "You have kids, don't you? You better watch them close. I know what it's like to lose someone I loved."

Mrs. Garza gasped, but she seemed incapable of controlling her brood. The boys were now softly cheering their sister. "You go, Bella" and other less pleasant taunts rang out. And I knew then that Bella Garza was stalking me. Somehow that was a comfort—what would a young girl do? I didn't think her words about the girls were real, but I wouldn't be taking any chances. My bet was that Bella wanted someone to save her from what she saw as her self-appointed duty.

I thrust the ham at Mrs. Garza but she shook her head. "They won't eat it. It will go to waste. Feed it to your husband and those girls, and treasure them. I...I apologize for my children. I can do nothing."

I took my ham and fled. The whole scene made me want to talk to Joe Mendez. His mother too had lost control of him, and he'd gone with a bad crowd, done bad things. A tangle with the law—and my intervention—set him on the right track. I wanted to ask him how we could reach out to Bella Garza and her family.

A few blocks way, I pulled over to the curb, pulled a Kleenex out of my purse and wept. I wasn't sure whom I cried for—Rosalinda, Bella, their mother, myself—but I cried until my eyes were puffy and red. Then I called Keisha and told her I was going home for the rest of the morning. I'd be in after lunch.

Mike was asleep, which gave me time to splash cold water on my face and try to restore my appearance at least a little. Instead of repeating my suggestion of the Grill, I fixed BLT sandwiches for lunch, and I think the smell of frying bacon brought Mike hobbling into the kitchen. One look at me, and he said flatly, "You've been crying. Is this all getting to be too much for you, with me unable to do anything?"

I shook my head. "No, no, that's not it. I just don't want to talk about it."

He boxed me into a corner with his walker. "We're going to talk about it. *Now.*"

"Let me get lunch on the table."

He moved slowly to the table and sat, his expression uncompromising. I wished he didn't know me so well.

When I put his beer and sandwich in front of him, he said, "Pull your chair up close to mine."

I got my own lunch and pulled my chair up.

Mike looked at my face again and said, "Wow! It must have been bad." He reached out a gentle hand and covered mine. This was the Mike I knew and loved, not the remote invalid I'd been living with lately. A good cry was worth it if it brought him out of his self-absorption.

"Tell me." It wasn't a command; it was a plea.

"Promise you won't get mad at me?"

That brought a questioning look. "Maybe exasperated?"

"I went to see Rosalinda Garza's family today—a mom, her twin sister, and three younger brothers. Oh, Mike, it was sad. None of them were in school, and the mom obviously had no control over them. Bella, that's the sister, tried hard to intimidate me, even threatened the girls, so I know she's the one who's been stalking me. But I think she'd love to be rescued from what she sees as her duty—revenge. I didn't even suggest she should be mad at Sonny Adams. I just left and brought my ham with me."

He opened his mouth in amazement and finally choked out, "Your ham?"

I looked down at my lap. "Yeah, I took a spiral-cut ham, figured they could use some food. I still think they could. But Bella refused it, and the mother said they wouldn't eat it and it would go to waste." I hesitated a moment. "I guess we'll have ham and potato salad Sunday."

He laughed this time. "We have ham sandwiches almost every day, so this ham is supposed to be a treat?"

"I won't let it go to waste."

"Good. But Kelly, you can't save the world. Just because you lucked out with Joe, you can't take on everyone's problems."

"I think Joe could help them. I'm going to talk to him about it Sunday."

"I'll be part of that discussion," he said, drinking the last of his beer. "Kelly, one of the reasons I love you is that you care so much about other people, but I won't let you put yourself or the girls in harm's way. I can't…I can't afford to take a chance. And it burns the hell out of me that right now I can't protect you. If I saw someone chasing you, the best I could do is holler for help."

I knew his male pride was hurt, but there was little I could say.

"Come on. I want to show you what I *can* do. Bother the dishes. Let them sit."

He clumped down the hall to the bedroom, almost banging his walker because he seemed in such a hurry. Once there, he threw back the covers on the bed.

"What are you showing me?" I asked, truly puzzled.

"What I can do with one bad leg," he answered with a smile.

"Mike? Should you? I mean, should we? I mean…."

"Stop talking and take off your clothes, woman."

It was amazing what he could do with one bad leg, and we stayed in bed until it was time for me to pick up the girls. If Keisha called, I didn't hear the phone.

****

Keisha didn't ask about my absence or about my visit to the Garzas except to say, "I guess you told Mike about going to the Garzas yesterday."

"Yes, I did. He understood…sort of. I'm going to see what Joe can do to help them."

"Help them? If I guess right, they're the ones stalking you, and you want to help them?"

As I saw it she shouldn't be surprised. This was kind of Keisha morality. You did what was right in the world for others, regardless of yourself. I'd long been impressed by that.

"You got it. It's the twin sister of the girl who died. She tried to be so hostile and threatening, but she was really just pitiful."

Keisha scoffed. "Pitiful, my foot. You watch out for her. Those girls know tricks you haven't even thought about. She'd as soon stick a knife in you as look at you. I went to school with girls like that, and I know them."

"Then how did you escape being like them?" I asked,

genuinely curious.

"My mama," was all she said, and it was enough.

Apparently Keisha morality went on hold when there was a threat to those she loved. She saw no benefit in trying to help the Garzas. To her mind, they were beyond help, and I was putting us all in danger.

"I don't believe that."

"Well, I do."

A frosty silence filled the office for quite a while, until at last I asked, "Keisha, can you bring your mom's good cheese grits on Sunday? We're having ham, and I'll make potato salad."

"What happened to burgers on the grill? If Mike can't grill, I can."

"Oh, I bought this ham. Just thought it would be a good idea."

"Garzas wouldn't take it, huh? So now we're eating their rejects. I'll bring grits but I think I'll also bring a layered Mexican dip—we might as well mix our cuisines, and I'm tired of sour cream and onion soup. Oh and I'm bringing José. Did I tell you that? That boy is growing on me." She looked coy, almost girlish. Then with the devil in her eye, she said, "I sure am glad I moved out of Mama's house."

She wouldn't dare mention my absence yesterday after that. I sat there linking José and layered Mexican dip in my mind. In truth, I was glad for a chance to know him. If I could only remember his real name.

Chapter Seven

Christian called after I got back from lunch. "Kelly, I kind of wandered on Magnolia today, in the area where Lattimore wants to build, and I went into a clock shop. Old guy named Otto Martin owns it. And he's madder than six demons. Making threats about Lattimore. Says he's too old to move and start over again and can't afford it. I want to meet with him...and you."

"Sure. I told you we need a meeting, and I'd like to include him. Did you ask Jim Price?"

"Yeah, he'll make himself available. Feels as strongly as we do. How about your office—not as many people around as at my office. What day's good for you?"

"Hmm, this is Friday. Could we do ten-thirty Monday morning? I checked and Tom's hearing with the zoning commission isn't until next Thursday."

"Great. I'll call Otto—he's really a great guy, you'll like him. You call Price and see if he can make it."

Jim Price was a lawyer in solo practice with an office on Magnolia. I imagined he'd make it if he weren't in court. When I called, he answered his own phone—I love lawyers like that—looked at his calendar, and said he'd meet us.

"Keisha, we're having a meeting of four people—plus you, of course—on Monday at ten-thirty. Can you take some petty cash that morning and get, oh, I guess doughnuts or whatever? And will you make a note to have fresh coffee?"

"Got it. What's this meeting about?"

"That shopping center Tom Lattimore wants to put in. Making plans to stop it."

"Guess the zoning regulations gonna be your weekend reading."

"Nope. I bet Jim Price is on top of that."

It turned out he was.

Shortly after that John Henry Jackson called. His voice boomed over the phone: "Little lady, I've talked to this Lattimore fellow, and I need to talk to you about this business on Magnolia Avenue. How about I take you to the Fort Worth Club for lunch on Tuesday—closed on Mondays, you know."

I didn't often get invited to the Fort Worth Club, a kind of upscale downtown club for businessmen. Most of Fort Worth's high society frequented it—and that didn't include me. "I'd appreciate a chance to talk, John Henry."

"Good. We'll meet at eleven-thirty. You know where to go?"

"Yes, I do. See you then."

****

Sunday night supper was delightful. By now my ham was a joke, and everyone teased me about it, which I tried to take gracefully, but it was a bit of a sore subject. Mom brought a chocolate meringue pie and a chocolate cake—she knew her granddaughters' addiction to chocolate. Claire brought sautéed green beans, fresh, with sliced almonds, declaring Megan and Liz loved them—and she brought enough for an army. Anthony and the boys arrived with a veggie and dip tray straight from a supermarket, and Theresa and Joe brought beer. It struck me what a difference a year made—Anthony frowned when he saw Theresa drink a beer, but after all she was a married woman now, and he said nothing.

The girls had set a festive buffet table. I taught them how to roll silverware, using those good sturdy paper napkins, and we had the clear plastic plates that I like. I'd splurged on flowers for the table, but even so Em accusingly said to Joe, "You didn't bring me balloons like you did last time."

"Do I have to bring you balloons every time I come to dinner?" he laughed.

"Yes," she said, flouncing away.

Theresa went after her, gave her a big hug, and asked about school. Em melted.

It was a bit cool outside, so we ate perched around the house, wherever we could find seats. Mike, as usual, sat in his big chair, and Maggie fixed him a plate, carefully cutting his meat for him, which I know amused him. He could, after all, still use a knife and fork, especially since he'd been ordered to exercise the fingers on his left hand. Maggie also heaped his plate with more food than any two men could eat, but he made a valiant effort.

José fit right in, although quietly. He talked some with Mike, but he never took his eyes off Keisha, and I saw them exchange a quick kiss in the kitchen. Em saw it too and screamed, "Keisha!" Keisha laughed and said, "Em, come give this boy a kiss. He deserves it." But Em turned shy. Joe jokingly told José that if one of them was to be called José so as to avoid confusion, it should be him since he was Mexican on both sides. José smiled and said, "I kind of like it as a nickname. Keisha gave it to me." As a couple they reminded me of Jack Spratt and his wife—José was taller than Keisha but not nearly as big. They made a handsome couple.

Soon after dessert everyone began to depart—work and school loomed for each of us the next day. I pulled Joe aside. "I know you and Theresa have early mornings, but could you stay a little bit? I want to talk to you."

"Sure, Miss Kelly. Whatever I can do."

Theresa took the girls off to get ready for bed and read a book, and I told Joe about the Garzas, without pausing for breath. Mike just sat and listened.

"So this lady, she's like my mom. Can't do anything with her kids. Right?"

"Right."

"I'm off Tuesday. I'll go see them. Those boys got to be in school. The girl?" He shrugged. "I don't know what I can do. But I'll try. Keisha may be right. You're not taking her seriously enough. And that would piss her off. Miss Kelly, please don't go up there again."

I evaded the asked-for promise.

"Thanks, Joe," Mike said. "I've been trying to tell Kelly."

"I haven't seen her following me since I went up there," I said defensively.

"Don't mean anything," Joe said. "Be foolish to think you scared her off with your visit." He rubbed his knuckles. "Tell you what, Miss Kelly, before I go see them, I'll check around and see what the word is, especially about the girl. Meantime, you be careful."

I really did think I had put an end to the stalking. I didn't worry about it as much as I should have.

****

Monday was my meeting with Christian, Jim Price, and the threatening Otto Martin. Threatening only because Christian said he made threats against Tom Lattimore. He turned out to be anything but. In fact, he was almost cherubic, with a slight hint of Old World charm about him. Short and chubby, balding with round cheeks and eyes that sparkled with an interest in life. When we were introduced, he took my hand and bowed low over it, almost but not quite kissing it.

I managed to stammer, "Charmed to meet you," which I thought was truly appropriate under the circumstances. Keisha, however, given the same treatment was speechless for the first time I could remember.

We pulled chairs up around my desk, which made me

feel that I was conducting the meeting, so I jumped in.

"Jim, how effective can the neighborhood association be in blocking this zoning change?"

"Depends, Kelly. We'll need petition signatures—ideally we should have a team go door to door. Not everyone will sign, but I think most will. We can't do that before Thursday."

"Pardon me, but I have a question. Can I be forced to sell my building? What if I just refuse?"

"The developers—whoever Lattimore is representing—will sweeten the pot."

"Sweeten the pot?" Otto asked. "I don't understand."

"Offer you an outrageous amount that you can't afford to turn down."

"I can't afford to accept anything. My building is all I have in the world. In the back, there's two rooms. That's where I live. My clock shop doesn't bring in enough to let me live anywhere else."

Forgetting why we were meeting, I asked, "Do you have a kitchen?"

He smiled. "I have a small refrigerator and a hot plate. It's all I need. I eat a lot of—what do you call it?—fast food."

"Oh, that's awful," I blurted out.

He shook his head. "No, I like my life. I don't want to change anything about it. I don't want to move if they offer me a house. I like where I am. My faithful customers know where to find me."

Jim Price was a kind and compassionate man. "If that's your home, they can't force you to move. The state has the right of eminent domain, but not private developers. I doubt they can prove public purpose or public necessity for a shopping mall."

"That's good," Otto said contentedly. "Because if they take my store, I'd have to kill Tom Lattimore."

I looked around as though I expected someone in authority—Buck or Mike, at the least—to be listening. "Uh, Otto…Mr. Martin, you mustn't ever say that aloud. It won't go any farther than this room, but if something were to happen to Mr. Lattimore, you'd be in big trouble."

He smiled. "I would be a happy man. I told the son of a bitch so."

Christian was convulsed behind his handkerchief, pretending to blow his nose, and Jim's mouth was quivering as he tried to quell his laughter. Keisha and I were simply amazed at this gentle man's open discussion of killing someone.

"I…I wouldn't want to have you as an enemy, sir," Jim said, finally controlling himself.

"Oh, I make a very good friend to people who treat me right."

I could not wait to tell Mike this story. We were having Otto Martin as a dinner guest soon—I'd see to it. And no hamburgers on the grill.

We finally settled down to tactics. Jim said we could have a meeting of the association next week and have petitions ready to be signed. At the meeting he'd ask for volunteers to walk the blocks. Then he asked Christian what his stake in this dogfight was, and Christian said, "I close titles for a lot of sales in Fairmount, people who want to live in a neighborhood that's kept its old charm. Build a shopping center, and it loses its appealing ambiance. Besides," he added, "I live in Fairmount. I want my kids to grow up in this kind of a neighborhood, where they can play outside safely and where people know them. I don't want an impersonal shopping center with its sales and crowds and parking lots."

"Fair enough," Jim said. "Though the nature of the store—if that's what he's really selling—may be more acceptable to the neighborhood than a Target would be.

That may hurt that argument." He turned to me.

"Kelly, I know your stake. And as of now, Mr. Martin, I certainly know yours. I can have my office draw up a petition, and I'll look into zoning laws. I think we can nip this thing in the bud."

I reported that John Henry Jackson, chair of the landmark commission, told me not to worry and that I was meeting him the next day. Christian said we had the full support of the League of Neighborhood Associations, and he passed out copies of the proposal Tom would present to the zoning commission. He had been able to secure the documents from the commission because Tom Lattimore was required to present paperwork a week in advance of the meeting. I saw one familiar name among the investors and wracked my brain to think who he was. A lawyer, I thought, and a courthouse pal of John Henry Jackson named Robert Lawler. Odd. Maybe Jackson would make him see the error of being involved in a project like this. The others were not major players in the Fort Worth commercial real estate market, in spite of what Tom had said about the investors being men with money and power in Fort Worth. They may have been, as Christian suggested, oil and gas men from anywhere. But, why, I wondered, would oil and gas men want to invest in a grocery market? I filed that one familiar name away; in fact, I wrote it on a scrap of paper and tucked it under the blotter on my desk.

The phone rang then, and even as I was signaling Keisha to ignore it, she got up and answered it. "No, she ain't in. May I take a message?" Then, loudly and laboriously, she asked, "Tom Lattimore? Does she have your number, sir?" He apparently replied in the affirmative, for she said, "I'll certainly ask her to call you as soon as she comes in."

Without a smile, she handed me a phone message slip. Then she addressed the group, "Mr. Price, I want to add my two cents. I got a stake too, and it goes beyond working for Kelly. I'm renting a small apartment in a big old Fairmount house. Mr. Otto, darlin', I got a small kitchen, so you just come over some evening, and I'll fix a dinner that'll knock your socks off."

He smiled and said thank you.

Keisha continued. "They're not too many neighborhoods where a black woman like me could rent in an Anglo-owned house and live on friendly terms with white, black, and Hispanic neighbors. I love it. I love this neighborhood. It's like no place else in the city, and we got to keep it."

Jim smiled. "We'll ask you to testify for the city council if it comes to that," he said.

Christian asked if any of us recognized any of the investors' names, and we all said no. I kept quiet about the one name I knew, though I'm sure Christian knew it too. We'd talk later.

"That's bad," he said. "They're not old Fort Worth, so they're not going to give a fig about our neighborhoods."

"A fig?" Keisha asked and laughed aloud.

Christian blushed. "Just a saying. You know what I mean."

"Yes sir, I surely do."

Jim looked at Keisha. "You and Mr. Martin make an eloquent case. It seems to me that this development goes against all zoning principles—it concentrates population in one specific area, it does not protect the rights of property owners or preserve a compatible neighborhood. I think we're in good shape, but we need to do some work."

"Then there's the battle over buildings on the national registry. They can't just tear down those buildings."

"That's when we go to the Landmark Commission," said Christian. "Kelly, you seem pretty sure of their support."

I nodded. "I'll get back to you after I meet with John Henry."

As they left, we congratulated each other on an optimistic outlook and were quite cheerful. Otto Martin bowed again to both me and Keisha and then waddled off behind Christian, who had brought him. I suspected he didn't own a car but would have easily walked from his shop to my office, a distance of over a mile.

Keisha, I could tell, was flattered to have been part of the meeting and to have had her two cents worth heard. I could sense it, but you'd never have known it from her words.

"You gonna call that jerk?"

"Excuse me?"

"Mr. Lattimore, as he so proudly calls himself. Can't even say Tom Lattimore like most folks. Reminds me of Mrs. Jerry North—we used to think her own first name was something she was so ashamed of, she wouldn't mention it."

Jo Ellen North had tried to kill me—after I found out her first name, but that's not the reason—and I didn't like being reminded of her.

"Yes," I said, waving the piece of paper. "I'll call Mr. Lattimore."

Then Keisha turned all dreamy. "Do you think I could teach José to do that?"

"Do what?"

"You know. Bow over my hand like that."

I swallowed a giggle. "Go ahead and try. I don't believe I'll mention it to Mike."

I had to swallow hard again when I called Tom Lattimore. Even though it was lunchtime, he was in his office and answered his own phone. "Tom, Kelly returning your call."

"Kelly, I was just about to go to lunch. Care to join

me? My treat."

"Oh, thanks, Tom. I was about to eat a sandwich at my desk"—my fingers were crossed which made that white lie okay— "What can I do for you?"

"I just got the plans for the shopping center, and I wanted to spread them out, see what you thought."

Tempting. I would be fighting the development with everything I had and seeing the plans could only add fuel to my fire. "I'd like to see them," I said and uncrossed my fingers—this was no lie. "Tell you what—let me go to that taco truck down the street, and get tacos for both of us. Spicy ground beef okay? We've got soft drinks in the office."

"Sounds great, although I may bring myself a beer. See you in twenty."

"If that means what I think it means, I'm going out for lunch," Keisha said.

"That's a good idea," I told her.

I called Mike to make sure he could manage lunch—he was getting around much better these days. "Sure, I can make a ham sandwich as good as you, but what's keeping you? I'll miss you."

"Don't tempt me, Mike Shandy. I have a business appointment, an important one. I'll tell you about it tonight."

"It better not be that Lattimore fellow," he said.

"Go fix your sandwich and have a beer." I scooted out the door, got the tacos, and hurried back to the office. Tom was waiting by the locked door.

"Sorry. Took longer than I thought."

"No problem, Kelly. I'm just really anxious to show you these plans. They're wonderful."

"Tom, you know I'm opposed to this. Why are you showing me the plans?"

"To convert you to my side."

"And why is that important?"

"Because you're an important voice for this community."

Contrary to traditional wisdom, Tom, flattery won't get you anywhere.

He couldn't contain his excitement, so we spread the plans out on the desk that once belonged to my ex-husband and was now bare and empty—I liked it that way. Just as I feared, the grocery store sat at the center back of a very large parking lot—really huge. The parking lot was broken into areas by plantings—trees, bushes, pampas grass— anything to break up the bare concrete. Smaller stores, with head-in parking, ringed the lot in front of the grocery store. To the side of the store was a structure labeled "Storage."

"What's that?"

"Oh, refrigerated storage. We'll disguise it with landscaping."

"I don't know any groceries that have adjacent cold storage facilities."

His enthusiasm made him seem boyish for a minute. "That's what so great about this, Kelly. Everything will be really fresh." He changed the subject. "See how neat the plantings are?"

"Yeah, they've really tried, Tom. But it's still a huge parking lot."

"Well, look at the stores on the side—we've got interest from a liquor store…."

I wanted to shout. "Oh, swell!" but I kept my mouth firmly shut.

"Then there's a shoe store, a local beauty salon—that should please folks, a local business, a well-known clothing chain. We'll get others."

"Except for the beauty salon, they're all national chains. What happens to the independent store owners who now operate on that property, like Otto Martin and his clock shop?"

"That old guy? Surely you can't be worried about him. Everything in his shop is so dusty, I bet he hasn't sold anything for a year. Besides he threatened me."

"Did you know he lives behind his store and has no other property? If you force him out, he'll be homeless." I looked for compassion; instead I got indignation.

"Lives behind his store? There ought to be a law against that! I bet that's grounds to take over his building."

"Tom, we're through here. Take your tacos and your beer and eat lunch somewhere else. I'm not interested in a shopping center, and I like Otto Martin a lot."

"Kelly, you can't be serious. Otto Martin threatened to kill me."

I was proud of my resolve. "Yeah, Tom, I'm very serious. And I told Otto not to say that aloud again."

He rolled up the plans, put a rubber band around them, said, "Keep your damn tacos," and fled.

I threw all the tacos, his and mine, in a wastebasket. I had no stomach for food.

The morning's meeting and Tom's plans made me want to visit my neighborhood. I drove down Magnolia to see firsthand the stores that would be affected by the development. One of the blocks he proposed to tear down had a two-level sidewalk—about halfway down the block, you had to climb an old set of concrete steps with a rickety iron pipe railing. They didn't build things like that anymore. I'd forgotten the beauty shop where they still back-combed hair and sprayed it stiff. A small irony: my company owned that building, and the beauty operator, a woman at least in her sixties with shoe-polish black hair, paid her rent faithfully the first of every month. Next door was the new yoga studio run by the young single mother—I had come to like Tanya. Was I supposed to put those two hard-working women out on the street? And one of the last old-fashioned shoe repair shops I knew about. I guess these days shoes are disposable: you just throw them out and buy a new pair.

Then I wandered through the neighborhood, looking at the houses—some Craftsman in good repair, other four-square Craftsman homes with beautiful gardens reaching out to the curb, a few brick homes, still other frame houses that seemed to need propping up, and a few with plywood nailed over the windows and doors. I looked at street signs and drove by one of the two elementary schools, down side streets that twisted and turned, and finally by my mom's house, now sporting a wonderful fall garden that she and Keisha had planted. We were getting there—many more houses in Fairmount were in good shape than not, but I felt in my bones that the shopping center would set back efforts to restore this glorious old neighborhood.

I was headed back to the office before I saw Bella's green Nova on my tail. So much for my faith in a fast conversion. Mike and Joe were right.

I didn't mention the tail to Keisha, but she looked out the window, saw the car, and said, "You hungry? I saw all those tacos in the trash. Bagged it and took it to the dumpster—don't like spicy food smellin' up my office."

I grinned, wanting to remind her that it was my office. "No, I'm not hungry. I have to get the girls soon. I'll fix a good dinner tonight."

"Such as?"

"The menu tonight is hamburger stroganoff, green beans, and salad," I said righteously.

"Lots of greens, that's good. 'Course that stroganoff has sour cream in it."

"Light sour cream."

Keisha laughed aloud. "Me? I'm fixin' fried chicken and cornbread and greens for José and Otto Martin. Gonna' be a southern feast. I get time I may make a chess pie."

"Otto Martin?"

"Of course. That poor old man needs company. Then maybe we can talk him outta killin' Tom Lattimore. Then again, maybe that's not such a bad idea. That man almost needs killin'." She turned back to her computer, cutting off the conversation.

Chapter Eight

"Mom," Em said from the backseat as we drove home from school that afternoon, "you forgot again."

Oh, Lord. What now? "What did I forget, Em?"

"Halloween. You always do."

She was right. Halloween always hit me like a brick had been thrown at me. "What do you want to be, Em?"

A big sigh. "I don't know. I've been a princess and a cat, and there's nothing left."

Such melodrama. I stifled a laugh, but Maggie jumped right in. "Em, I have my ballet clothes—I bet they'd just fit you now, even the shoes. You could be a ballerina in a tutu!"

Em considered. "It's pink, isn't it?"

"Yep, it's pink. When we get home, pull it out so Em can try it on."

That afternoon the green car stayed behind us from the school to the house and then sped away. I didn't mention it, but Maggie saw it. "I'm not walking Gus this afternoon. I'll throw the ball for him in the yard."

"Okay. Just clean up any mess he makes."

Another sigh, this time from my oldest child. I made a mental note to buy a pooper-scooper.

The girls greeted Mike, who was working at his computer on the dining room table. Each day he was getting around better, using the walker a little less, especially if I was nearby for him to balance on. He still hobbled, and he still went to therapy three times a week, but as he improved physically I could have drawn a chart of his emotional improvement.

I gave him a kiss and asked how his work was going—he was back at work on his history of fallen policeman in Fort Worth.

"Good. I'm up to 1900, but I'm thinking of going back and including peace officers of Tarrant County from the time of its incorporation."

Sounded deadly dull to me, but it would keep him occupied.

"Conroy's taking me to lunch tomorrow. That new burger place—what's it called? Smashburger. He says just to visit but I suspect he has more on his mind."

"Good for you. I'm going to lunch with John Henry Jackson at the Fort Worth Club." I waited for a reaction, but there was none.

I sat down across the table, bursting to tell him about my meeting with Christian and Jim Price, my non-lunch with Tom Lattimore, and my curiosity about my lunch date the next day with John Henry Jackson. I knew he'd love the tale of me throwing the tacos in the trash and Keisha bagging them. I was just getting to the good part, where I told Tom to take his tacos and go when the girls came into the room.

"What do you think, Mike?" Maggie asked. "Doesn't she make a good ballerina?"

Em twirled in sort of a pirouette that Maggie must have just shown her.

Mike beamed. "You'll be great at ballet, Em. I didn't know you want to take lessons."

Maggie gave him a withering look. "Not lessons. This is her Halloween costume. Mom's gonna get her a sparkly mask."

News to me.

Mike turned quiet and then looked at the girls. "Maggie, Em, I don't think there will be any trick or treating this year. I can't take you, and I don't want your mom doing it."

Em began to pout but Maggie asked sensibly. "What about Keisha?"

Mike pondered that. "I'd rather have a man take you."

Em said, "Joe!" while Maggie suggested, "Keisha's new boyfriend, José." I sat silently thinking that was a truly sexist remark that I didn't expect from Mike. I suppose he was thinking in terms of physical strength, but the remark still grated on my feminist nerves a bit.

"Let me talk to both of them," I said, "and see what I can do. Maggie, you never told me what you want to be."

"I think I'll just pick out a mask when we go to get one for Em." Her world-weary tone implied that she was too old for a costume, and I didn't tell her that adults had costume parties. "You girls go along. Maggie, Gus needs to go out, and Em, you put on play clothes and be very careful of Maggie's ballet things. Hang the tutu up carefully. I'm talking to Mike."

"Can we listen?" It was Maggie, the ever curious.

"No. It's nothing that will interest you."

Mike repeated my words but added, "Your mom really stood up for herself this morning. I'm proud of her."

"Then I am too," Em said and came over to give me a big kiss.

"What did you do, Mom?" Maggie asked.

"I didn't let a man bully me into doing something I didn't want to do. And I ended up throwing his lunch—and mine—in the wastebasket. Of course, Keisha emptied it. Said she didn't like the smell of tacos in the office."

"You didn't tell me that part," Mike said, laughing. "Now tell me about your meeting this morning."

"Not much to it. Jim Price is going to call an association meeting and talk to the people at the League of Neighborhoods, and Christian is going to research zoning laws and the like. He had a copy of what Tom will present to the zoning commission. But, Mike, the most adorable man was there."

His eyebrows shot up.

"No, not that kind of adorable. He's probably close to seventy, short and a bit pudgy with chubby cheeks and a bald head. He owns a small clock shop where Tom wants to build his shopping center. And he lives behind the clock shop—says he has a hot plate and a refrigerator, and that's all he needs. He eats out a lot, which I thought was kind of sad. Keisha's fixing him dinner tonight at her apartment."

"I can see we're going to adopt this man," Mike smiled. "You aren't matchmaking for your mom, are you?"

"Heavens no. She wouldn't be interested. I don't think he's ever married, and I bet he's shy as can be around women. He's sort of Old World courtly—but the funny part is that he's dead serious that if this development goes through he'll have to kill Tom Lattimore. Sort of an honor thing with him."

Mike drew his breath in sharply. "Girls, go do as your mother asked you to." As soon as they were out of hearing range, he said, "Kelly, that's hardly a story to tell in front of the girls. And probably you shouldn't tell me. If anything happens to Lattimore, I'm honor bound to report what I heard."

"We told him that it was dangerous to make empty threats. I don't think he considers it an empty threat—he's that serious—but I don't think he'd ever do it."

"Well, I'm kind of curious to meet him," Mike admitted.

"Good. I'll invite him for Sunday supper. Maybe with Christian and his wife. You know, enlarge our circle of friends."

"Why not Buck and Joanie?" he asked.

I still had a hard time getting used to the fact that Buck Conroy, once my nemesis, was now my friend and mostly on my side. And I had a harder time believing he'd married Joanie, nursed her through a pregnancy with another man's child, and was now happily settled as a family man. Joanie had been my best friend until the night she confessed my ex-husband might be the father of her child. We were still friends, but there was a rift there that took a long time to heal.

"I suppose we could."

I guessed that meant I wasn't inviting Christian and his wife and baby but I was inviting Buck and Joanie along with MacKenzie, who was now, I thought, at least two. I only hoped Otto wouldn't say anything about killing Lattimore in front of Buck.

I changed the direction of the conversation. "I've been thinking it's time for you and me to have dinner at Lili's some night soon. Keisha would babysit, I'm sure."

"I think your mom feels she hasn't been around much. Why not ask her, and have Keisha on standby in case Nana gets into trouble."

"Good idea. Saturday night?"

"You have a date, milady."

****

The next day I dressed with care for my lunch with John Henry Jackson, but I didn't go so far as to wear a skirt. These days you could go anywhere in Fort Worth in pants, even the staid old Woman's Club which had required skirts for years. I wore a muted gray windowpane plaid pantsuit with a silk blouse with ruffles that spilled over the lapels of the jacket, black pumps, and carried a small black purse. To add color, I draped a fuchsia silk scarf around my neck. When I got ready to leave the house, Mike whistled and then said in a threatening tone, "You meeting that Lattimore fellow again?"

"Nope. I told you. John Henry Jackson, chair of the Historic Landmark Commission and a former city council member, is taking me to the Fort Worth Club no less." I twirled in front of him as though I wore a frothy chiffon skirt.

He whistled again then asked, "Do I know John Henry Jackson?"

"Don't think so. He's a title lawyer and a darn good one, though you'd never know it to look at him. I'm not so sure about his interest in preservation, but I'll take lunch at the Fort Worth Club."

He raised a questioning eyebrow, and I elaborated. "He's overweight, his clothes are spotted. You'd think he's one of those lawyers hanging around waiting to be assigned a public defender case. But you'd be wrong. He used to be on the city council. Got angry over something and, as they say, took his huff and departed in it. Then he lobbied the council to make him chair of the commission."

Mike grinned. "Sounds harmless to me."

"No competition for you," I said as I kissed him goodbye.

John Henry was at the club when I arrived, with a martini in front of him. He rose gallantly while the maitre d' seated me, not an easy matter for John Henry. He carried close to 300 pounds on maybe a six-foot frame; he was balding, with wispy gray hair flying in all directions around the sides of his head. He wore suspenders and an old-fashioned watch fob stretched across his middle, and he had a tendency to fiddle nervously with the watch. He wasn't really checking on how much time he'd spent with you, but it gave that impression. His coat and tie were often spotted just a bit, and he wheezed easily when he'd exerted himself at all. He was not a graceful figure. Once seated again, he raised his glass and asked, "Will you join me?"

"In a martini? No, thanks. But I'd love a glass of chardonnay." *What the heck? I could have wine at lunch on an occasion—and lunch at the Fort Worth Club was an occasion for me.*

John Henry urged me to order the filet mignon with roasted fingerling potatoes or the salmon filet with goat cheese mashed potatoes, but it all sounded too heavy, and I stuck with a tuna salad plate. Someday my tombstone may read, "Died from eating too much tuna salad." John Henry ordered the steak.

When my wine came, we toasted to the preservation effort in Fort Worth and chitchatted about light things. He asked about the girls, and I asked about his practice. John Henry was a bachelor, so I couldn't inquire about family. We agreed that all was well in both our worlds.

Finally, he got down to business. "I've met with this Tom Lattimore, and I think we can negotiate."

Negotiate? Alarm signals went off in my brain. "Negotiate how?"

"Well, Lattimore is sensitive to the nature of the community, but he's also sold on this project and the ways it would be a benefit, draw traffic to Magnolia."

"Magnolia already has enough traffic," I interrupted.

John Henry raised his hand. "Hear me out. He understands about the significance of those historic buildings, and he's willing to consider adaptive re-use."

"Adaptive re-use?" I looked around to see if I'd shouted and heads had turned my way. "How's he going to adapt those old buildings to a modern large-scale grocery store?"

"He has a pretty good plan that would incorporate the buildings, making them into specialty boutiques and building the larger store behind them, with parking to the side. He's eliminated the satellite stores. You have to admit, Kelly, he's really going a long way to be accommodating." Just then the waiter approached with our lunches, and John Henry waved his hand in the air dismissively. "No more business talk. Let us enjoy our food."

After we finished our entrees, he began fiddling with

his watch, but he invited me to have coffee and dessert. I declined the dessert but accepted the coffee. He had none, and when I was about halfway through my cup, he stood up, indicating lunch was over.

I thanked him for lunch as we left the formal dining room, but I couldn't resist adding one question: "John Henry, what about the people who will be displaced from their small businesses?"

That hand waved again. "Not my concern," he said. "I'm a preservationist, not a social worker."

I was stunned, and we rode the elevator to the parking garage in silence.

****

Mom readily agreed to babysit Saturday night—"I've been missing those girls!"—and Keisha agreed she'd be on call. "José and me, we'll probably stay home. He likes my cooking real well," she said. "We had a good time with ol' Otto last night. That man can eat—and he can tell a story. You know he's had that clock shop forty years—learned clock making from his German daddy. Had all of Fort Worth's bigwigs in there, including Mr. Amon Carter himself. José's kind of quiet, so it was good to have Otto talkin' his head off. I think he's lonely."

"I'll invite him to dinner this weekend, but Mike and I have a real date on Saturday. We're going to Lili's."

"I'll be sure José and me don't go there. I'm tryin' to learn to cook Mexican food the way his mom does. She's gonna give me lessons, but I bet she don't write a thing down. Just like my mama."

"So you've met his mother? This is getting serious."

She just patted her upswept hairdo and preened a bit. Then, as she does, she cut off conversation by turning to her computer. "I got work to do," she said, implying I should get to my work.

On Wednesday, Mike was having lunch with Conroy

again so I called Claire. She was delighted to make plans, and we decided to go to Carshon's, the neighborhood deli—okay, one of the few in the city. I didn't eat there often, but I always loved it when I did.

"I'll pick you up about 11:30," I said. Lunch with Claire would be as much a courtesy call as friendship. She'd recently referred three friends to me who wanted to move from newer parts of the city to Fairmount. So far I'd found a house for one of them, and I had my eye on one that fit another's requirements. Matching people and houses is part of the fun of my business.

Keisha broke the silence in the office. "Forgot, Kelly. Did you know José is getting reassigned to Mike's Fairmount beat?"

My heart skipped. A succession of officers has filled in since Mike's accident but no one had the beat permanently. Was this what Conroy wanted to talk to Mike about? "Effective when?"

"Tomorrow night. He's excited about it, and he wants to talk to Mike about it, see what he needs to know and do."

Impulsively, I said, "I'm going to invite Buck and Joanie and Otto for Sunday dinner. Why don't you and José join us? If he's got Mike's beat, he should be off on Sundays."

"Sounds good. Tell me what to bring."

I changed the subject. "Do you know if he'll have to work Halloween? Mike won't let the girls go trick or treating without a man along."

"A man? What's got into his head? I can handle any man…and certainly any little girl that drives a green Nova, like that one sitting across the street."

I glanced out and there was Bella. If I called Conroy, she'd be gone—she seemed to have that kind of radar. Besides, there's no law against sitting in a parked car. I couldn't prove harassment, though her plan seemed to be working well. She was definitely getting on my nerves—and causing discord in my household.

"You can try to tell him, but I doubt he'll listen. Joe Mendez is supposed to call me tonight, and I'll talk to him."

Claire and I had a delightful lunch. We split a Reuben, and when she asked, "So what else is new?" she let herself in for it. I spilled all my troubles about Bella Garza tailing me. Her reaction was not the immediate horror some people would have had. Claire was too controlled for that. Instead, she said, "That girl-child needs to have her ears boxed—or her bottom swatted *hard!*"

I told her Mike and Joe thought the girl was beyond that kind of discipline and told her about my visit to the Garza home.

"No wonder there are so many uneducated kids who can't earn a living," she said. "That's the answer to the welfare problem—education. But you can't convince the powers that want to cut education funding. It's enough to make me want to move to Canada."

"They have similar problems, I think. Besides, I have another story to tell."

Claire waited, and I rattled off the Tom Lattimore story, ending with throwing all those tacos in the trash. She laughed and laughed until she cried and people at other tables turned to look at us. "That really is wonderful, Kelly. I knew of course that you had it in you—I saw you face down a drunken Jim Guthrie, with a gun in his hand. I have a message for Tom Lattimore, the little twerp: don't underestimate Kelly O'Connell." She fished for a Kleenex and wiped her eyes.

As we left, I said impulsively, "Come by for a drink tonight. I'll get out some cheese and crackers. Bring the girls."

"They're so wrapped up in their studies and activities

that I almost never see them. Megan does have a steady beau, and I think I like him. Name's Brandon Waggoner, an old West Side family. Jim would be pleased. She's only a sophomore, so it's way too early for her to settle down, but for the time being Brandon is a good choice. I've been wondering if he's descended from the rancher—you know, Tom Waggoner."

"You forget I'm a northerner, and no, I don't know, but tell me if you find out there's a connection. See you about five tonight."

Claire came bearing a bottle of merlot for herself and Mike, because she knew he liked red wine. For me, chardonnay. I put out a plate of cheese and crackers—that good rattrap cheese I just love—and we settled down to talk. Mike seemed genuinely glad to see her. But almost as soon as I sat down, the phone rang. When I saw it was Joe Mendez, I excused myself and took the call in the bedroom.

Chapter Nine

"Miss Kelly, I got news, but it isn't all good. Of course my friends—uh, contacts—are all older than Bella Garza, but they know her by reputation and they hear things. They tell me she's tough, and she's out for revenge. Brags about stalking you, scaring you. I don't know if she'll do more than that, but I wouldn't take a chance. The mom is absolutely no help—no control over the kids."

"What about the boys?"

"The thirteen-year-old and the fifteen-year-old, Michael and Alex, are both on probation. But if that's the case, they should be sent to the alternative school. I know—I been on probation. It don't mean you can sit home all day and watch TV. I told the mom she needs to call the school, but I'll check in a couple of days. If she hasn't done anything, I will."

"What about the older boy?"

"She calls him Ben. He's a dropout, but he isn't working either. I'm going by one day and take him—oh, I don't know, maybe bowling. Talk to him about responsibility and helping his mom. It might work, probably won't."

"Joe, if he earns his GED, like you did, I'll pay his first semester tuition at the county college."

"Miss Kelly, you can't do that!"

"I can. Now I'm only sorry I didn't do it for you."

"No, no. You gave me the will to go there. I'm proud I did it myself, but I thank you for the shove." I heard him chuckle.

"Thanks, Joe. I appreciate what you're doing. I'd like

to see those boys helped—the whole family in fact. Any mention of a dad?"

"In prison—for a long time apparently. Don't know what for."

"Well, as for Bella, I don't know what to do. I guess I'll just keep being careful, but she's beginning to get on my nerves."

"That's what she wants, Miss Kelly. She wants you to get fed up and let your guard down. Next time I have a day off, I think I'll stalk her and corner her so I can talk to her."

"Joe, I don't know how to thank you."

"Theresa and me, we owe you everything. I do whatever I can."

"Joe, one more question—on a different topic. Will you be free on Halloween? Mike has this ridiculous notion that neither Keisha nor I can take the girls trick-or-treating. He wants a man with them."

I could practically hear him shake his head over the phone. "No, Miss Kelly. We have a Halloween party at the YMCA. But Theresa can bring the girls. They'd have fun."

"Hmm. I'll run it by Mike before I mention it to them. He's taking fatherhood really seriously."

"Good for him. I'll be in touch. Bye, Miss Kelly."

By the time I got back to the living room, Claire was saying it was time for her to leave. "Mike and I had a good visit. We agree on some things—like you being careful."

"I will." No need to go into Joe's report right here. I gave Claire a hug and said, "Let's not wait so long to get together."

Mike stood to walk Claire to the door—with his walker. "Kelly may be free more often from now on at lunch time," he said. "Buck Conroy wants me to take a desk job in the precinct and study for the detective exam."

I would have thrown my arms around him, except for fear of sending us both crashing over the end table he was standing by. "Mike, that's wonderful."

"Maybe. Time for me to get out of the house. I'll just be answering phones but I'll be back in the midst of things." He smiled a bit. "And I can make sure Kelly isn't meddling in police work."

I raised a hand as if to smack him, but he grabbed it and kissed it.

"That's good news, Mike. I hope it works out for you."

"Thanks." And he actually hugged her.

After Claire left, I asked, "Have you decided she isn't responsible for Jim Guthrie's fatal accident?"

"No, that doubt will always be in the back of my mind. But the system has worked. I have to be satisfied."

We sat at the table, sipping wine. "Mike, are you really pleased at Conroy's offer?"

"Yeah, I am. It does mean telephone duty—but not like 911. And I'll study for the exam. Bottom line, though, is Buck says they'll probably never put me back on patrol. I couldn't run hard or fast enough if I had to." He hung his head. "It's disappointing, because I really liked being on the streets, and because it means I'll never do those triathlons. All because some idiot ran a stop sign... and killed an innocent girl, besides messing up my leg."

It was time to tell him about Joe's findings of the day, and I did.

His first reaction was predictable. "Kelly, I want you to take the course, get your CHL, and carry a small handgun in your purse all the time."

"Mike, you know I'm opposed to that. I'd shoot myself before I shot the bad guy—or, uh, girl."

"Not if you had training. I'll make some compromises with you but this isn't one of them. I can't quite see arming you with a knife. I'm afraid then you would get hurt worse than the other...uh...person."

We both knew who we were talking about and that she

was probably proficient with a knife, her weapon of choice.

"As for Joe, bully for him for taking on the Garza family. But Kelly, remember that's not your fight. You have me and the girls to take care of, and now I'm sure you've taken on this Otto Martin. You simply can't save the world."

"I can try."

He smiled and held out his arms, and I walked into them, sitting carefully on his lap for fear of hurting him.

Maggie bounded into the room then stopped short. "I caught you smooching!"

I laughed, "Yes, you did. Is that so bad?"

"No, it's kinda nice. Mom, did you ask Mike if we could go to the YMCA Halloween party?"

"Maggie Spencer, how did you know about that? Were you listening in on my conversation with Joe?"

"Only that part of it," she said, hanging her head.

Mike was stern. "I should say no, you can't go because you did what you know you're not supposed to. You listened in on someone else's phone call. That's eavesdropping, and it's wrong. I'm tempted to let Em go and keep you at home."

Tears puddled in her eyes, but she was determined not to cry, big as she was. Mike gently pushed me aside and pulled Maggie into his arms. "Promise never to do that again?"

She nodded.

"You can go, only if Theresa takes you."

She threw her arms around him and hugged tight. That made *me* teary.

After the girls were tucked in bed that night, Mike and I sat close together on the couch, not talking about much, just enjoying being together. But we both decided we were really tired.

As I turned out the light in the front window, I saw the

green Nova across the street. *Doesn't that child ever sleep?* I left the porch light on and checked the alarm but didn't mention the car to Mike, just snuggled a little closer to him in bed.

As I drifted off, I made a note of another chore for the next day—call Tanya, the young single mother whose yoga studio was threatened by Lattimore's commercial development. I should have started yoga two months ago. Okay, I should have been doing it all along—I needed exercise, and I hadn't been getting it. Claire was kind to offer but I wanted to support Tanya, and I would feel guilty taking charity from Claire.

Noises in the driveway wakened me in the early morning hours. The motion-sensing lights came on and the driveway was flooded with light. And someone was yelling, something that sounded like, "Yippee!" over and over. I sat up in bed but Mike was already up and out of bed, this time using his walker for speed, his service revolver in his hand. If I hadn't been so scared, I'd have realized he made a ridiculous image wearing only boxer shorts.

I heard the front light switch click off and then the front door open. Good for Mike—he left the alarm system on. Within seconds, its sirens began blaring outside and inside.

The girls were in our bed before I could blink. They had heard too many things go bump in the night during their young lifetimes, and they were easily scared. Now they both had their hands over their ears.

"Mom, what is happening?" Maggie whispered.

"I don't know, but Mike will tell us," I whispered back. Then aloud, "We don't have to whisper. No one can hear us, and whispering just makes us more afraid."

"But I *am* afraid," Em wailed.

"Mike will keep us safe," I said.

Flashing lights filtered through the blinds, and I knew

the police were here. Mike clumped down the hall to get a pair of pants and commanded, "You three stay right here. Go to sleep."

As if we could!

He was gone forever, or so it seemed. Finally I heard him click on the porch light, set the alarm, lock the door, and come haltingly down the hall, without the speed he'd shown getting out. Dispiritedly, he sat on the edge of the bed, commanded the girls to look the other way, and then slid out of his shoes and pants and crawled into the bed.

"Girls, you may sleep with us, but you best sleep on the other side of your mother. I need her as a barrier between me and your kicks."

They didn't say a word but settled down quietly.

"Mike?"

"She slashed the tires on both cars. Conroy's sending someone to get me in the morning. Can you get Keisha to get the girls to school while you call Triple A about getting the tires changed and Dave Summers about insurance?"

"Sure." *So our girl did have a knife. Guns weren't her style. Probably smart of her. And probably something she learned fighting in the streets.* I wondered if she had scars I hadn't noticed.

Mike fell asleep instantly—how I envied him that ability—and on the other side of me the girls slept, comfortably curled about each other. I lay awake, dreading the future.

****

When I called Keisha early the next morning, she reminded me—as she had twice for the last week—that the zoning commission would hold an open hearing that morning on Tom Lattimore's petition for a variance. There went Triple A—I'd have to deal with the tires in the afternoon. Mike protested that since it was his first day back at work, sort of, he couldn't attend the meeting, and I understood.

Keisha and I delivered the girls to school, went to Starbucks, ran by the office, and were in the zoning commission hearing by nine o'clock. I'd been in zoning commission hearings before, though never over a huge commercial property. My interests had been for remodeling houses, preserving the neighborhood, small stuff. But I knew that the men and women who sat impassively behind that long table were just people like everyone else, albeit with more knowledge of the zoning laws and regulations. Zoning variation requests looked like they were written in a foreign language until you understood the code. In this case I understood only too well: Tom wanted a change from light commercial to heavy. Accordingly the commission had sent notices to property owners within 300 yards of the property to be affected, and these property owners were invited to be present at the hearing and to speak in an orderly and brief fashion. It would, I knew, be a long morning.

Tom presented his case, stressing economic benefits to the area, increased availability of affordable goods in the satellite stores as well as fresh and healthy food in the new anchor store, and surprisingly, neighborhood support for the project. He brought forth a string of witnesses—the taco shop owner testified that he supported the development because it promised him better quarters for his business; one or two other small businesses near the site echoed that sentiment. Had Tom "forgotten" to tell them about the new plan calling for adaptive re-use? Or was he simply hoping to push the original plan through with this commission and deal with John Henry later? A couple of owners of residential properties behind the site testified that they would welcome the convenience of nearby shopping, and several residents welcomed the idea of a gourmet shopping center in the neighborhood. With a final sweeping gesture, Tom laid his petitions before the commission members.

When testimony from the opposition was allowed, pandemonium broke loose with people clamoring to testify—including me. I glanced at Tom and saw his face pale.

The chair of the commission announced that ten people, chosen at random, would be allowed to speak and requested all who wanted to testify to stand. I stood, and I prayed that Otto Martin would be chosen. He wasn't—in retrospect that was a good thing. He might have repeated his threat on Tom's life. Keisha was chosen, and so was I, along with Tanya who owned the yoga studio, and Christian. I didn't recognize the others. Keisha gave the same impassioned plea she had at the meeting in our office; Christian spoke in business terms about the impact of the neighborhood, especially traffic congestion, which would affect not only the immediate area but almost the whole of Magnolia; Tanya told her own personal story in a most effective way; and I began with Otto Martin's story then moved into the real estate implications. I talked so long that the chair cut me off with a curt, "That will do. Thank you."

The other testimonies were along the same lines, dwelling upon preserving the neighborhood ambiance, the friendly familiar comfort of Fairmount as a neighborhood. There was no reading the commissioners' faces, but I noticed Tom running a nervous finger around his collar.

Jim Price was offered a chance to speak as chair of the neighborhood association, and he rose to say affirmatively, "Ladies and gentleman, I am firmly opposed to this project. I do feel, in addition, that the neighborhood has been blindsided. The petitioner had much more advance knowledge than the opposition, and we respectfully request a postponement to give us time for a neighborhood meeting and to circulate petitions."

Tom tried to be flippant. "Don't bother. Everyone's

already signed my petition."

Jim matched him in tone. "Oh, I imagine we can find one or two folks who haven't signed yet."

The chair of the commission asked, "Mr. Price, would a month be sufficient?"

"Yes, sir. I imagine we can get a lot done in a month."

"So granted," and he banged his gavel on the table. "Next item."

Tom left as soon as the chair announced the delay, but his face looked ashen.

It took me the rest of the day to get all the tires changed on our cars. Keisha picked up the girls, gave me a few messages from the office, and left us. By then, I was anxious about Mike and his day. I knew better than to call, and I knew doubly sure he wouldn't want me picking him up. So I set the girls to doing their homework and put myself to making a cheeseburger meatloaf, one of Mike's favorites.

He came in a little after five, followed by Conroy, whose first words were, "Can I please have a beer?"

"Not before I kiss Mike," I said.

"Oh, sheesh! Newlyweds."

Mike wrapped his arms around me, holding me tight to keep his balance, and gave me a sound kiss.

"How was it?" I asked.

His smile was rueful. "Even sitting at a desk, I missed my naps. I'm really out of shape."

"I made him get up frequently," Conroy said, "and I made him do some of his stretches and exercises."

"In the station headquarters?" I was incredulous, and Mike just hung his head. I knew it had embarrassed him.

"Yep. Now about that beer. I got other news."

I fetched a beer, feeling like a barmaid. Mike had shaken his head "No" when I asked him.

Settling himself on the couch, with the girls as a

spellbound audience, Conroy came close to putting his feet on the coffee table, thought better of it, and said, "We picked up your girl today."

My girl?

"We picked up Bella Garza." His tone was impatient, as though I should have known instantly.

"Where?"

"Dump of a bar on Hemphill. Took her in and fingerprinted her, booked her, the whole works. Suspicion of vandalism. Underage drinking—she's nineteen as you know. Then we let her go. Any judge would throw the case out of course, but we wanted her to know we have our eye on her."

"She seem impressed?" I asked.

Mike joined in. "Not the way I heard it. That girl's got a dirty mouth, and she let loose on them."

"All talk and no show," Conroy said, taking a deep pull at his beer.

"I don't trust that," Mike said. "It's my family whose safety is at stake."

"We're watching her, Mike. I told you that. Kelly, can you keep a record of when and where you see her? Sort of a log."

"Sure."

"Mom?" Maggie interrupted, and I started to shush her, until she said, "That old green car is outside again, right in front of our house."

Conroy jumped to his feet and ran to the window, only to exclaim, "The little bitch has a lot of nerve!"

I wanted to cover the girls' ears, but it was too late.

When Conroy came back to the couch, he looked disturbed. "There were two people in that car. She was driving, wearing her damned baseball cap, but there was a guy in the passenger seat. She's got help. I don't like it." He picked up his beer.

"Girls, don't you need to finish your homework in your rooms?" I asked.

Maggie stood firm. "No way I'm missing this."

Mike looked at her, considered his options, and said nothing. We were all baffled, trying to figure out what new dimension Bella's accomplice brought to the situation.

Finally Mike said, "I'd like to rush out there and grab both of them."

"Fine," I retorted, "and break your good leg?"

He grunted. "There was a time when I could have done it."

I put my hand over his.

Conroy was on the phone, muttering and mumbling. When he clicked off his cell phone, he said, "Patrol car'll be here in a minute. Check them out for loitering. He can tell us about the passenger." Sometimes I underestimated Buck Conroy.

Sure enough, a police car pulled up almost instantly, did that little squawk that tells someone they're there but doesn't warn them blocks away. Conroy went strutting out the door, and the girls and I rushed to the window.

"I wish you wouldn't do that," Mike said. "Don't let them see that you're interested."

"But I *am* interested," Em wailed. "I don't like that girl."

Mike appealed to me with his eyes, and I said, "Girls, stand away from the window, to the side where you can't be seen." I peeked out the window in the door. We all saw the officers drag the girl and a boy out of the car, make them spread their arms and legs against the car, and pat them down.

"Oh, for gosh sake," I cried. "Surely they don't have weapons."

Mike gave me one of those looks. "You a seasoned officer by now?" and I subsided. They probably did have knives of one sort of another.

They actually took those kids away, leaving the car in front of our house. That made it hard for me to sleep—or I thought it would. But cuddled next to Mike, I slept soundly. Next morning the green car was gone, and Mike said they had booked Bella and a twenty-year-old male named Ben Smith (really?) on charges of loitering and suspicion of vandalism. Then they let them go on their recognizance. It was the best they could do, he said.

"That's her brother," I said. "Ben Garza."

I was back to worrying about Bella Garza.

Chapter Ten

Dinner at Lili's was hardly the quiet, only-the-two-of-us evening that I had envisioned. Everyone from the owner to half the customers stopped to greet Mike, tell him how glad they were to see him, and ask how he was doing. In between, we managed to order house salads with that good blue cheese dressing and our favorite entrée, the veal piccata. We lingered over a second glass of wine but turned down dessert and coffee and hurried home to the girls. In the car, Mike confessed, "It makes me a little nervous to leave the girls with your mom. The three of them seem pretty defenseless."

"Don't underestimate the new Nana," I replied, but I too was glad to be back home. We'd had our date night for the foreseeable future.

Sunday night supper with Otto Martin was a delight. I had decided to balance things out by inviting Mom, ignoring Mike's gibes about matchmaking for her. Mom was far too sophisticated for Otto Martin, especially since she'd rebuilt her life these days. She was always well groomed, sort of like Claire, in outfits instead of the haphazardly thrown together things I wore. She kept her hair just lightly blonde and well cut. She was at the church all the time, but she also dined out at nice restaurants—Lili's, Nonna Tata, Ellerbe, The Tavern, Patrizio's. She had done what I prayed for—gotten a life for herself. We didn't see her much, which was and wasn't okay.

Mom brought an Italian cream cake—an elaborate affair of whipped cream, rum flavoring, coconut, and cream cheese that made Mike whisper to me, "She's trying to make an impression on Otto."

In truth, she wasn't. These days I marveled at my mom. She had changed so much from the timid woman I'd moved out of her longtime home in Chicago. She was self-confident and an interesting conversationalist—both of which had been missing before.

I had warned Mike that José was taking over his neighborhood patrol, so he was prepared and appropriately gratified when José asked for advice, places and people he should know about, places he should particularly keep an eye on. They went off in a corner and talked quietly, though I heard Mike tell him about a couple of supposed crack houses he should keep an eye on and one house where he suspected there were too many unattached women who might just be running an illicit business. It made me wonder again about the neighborhood I was bringing my girls up in, but my corner of Fairmount seemed so safe and secure.

When Buck and Joanie arrived, Buck quickly took over the professional conversation, giving José all kinds of complicated advice about the neighborhood. The only sensible thing I heard was, "Watch for a battered green Nova and call me when you see it. Drive by here often."

"I plan to walk a lot," José said.

"You can't walk this entire neighborhood."

"No, but I can walk sections of it and keep my mike on." José stood up for himself with surprising independence, and I silently cheered. Keisha poked me in the ribs and winked.

Joanie was Joanie, wrapped up in McKenzie, though she was sweet about letting the girls play with her and letting Maggie give her a sippie cup of milk and hold her on her lap. Then Joanie dropped her bombshell.

"I'm pregnant again, and this one is Buck's baby."

Buck smiled triumphantly and bragged, "This one's gonna be a boy. You watch and see." I was glad McKenzie wasn't old enough to understand. She'd feel like a second-class citizen, and I hoped this new baby, boy or girl, wouldn't overshadow her. We all congratulated them. Privately I thought Joanie was about to have her hands full with babies little more than two years apart.

While Keisha and I put out the buffet on the kitchen counter—another ham because the last one had actually been such a hit there was hardly any left for sandwiches, potato salad, cheese grits, and a relish platter for fresh vegetables—Mom and Otto were off in a corner. I couldn't hear what they were saying, but Mom was laughing and Otto was talking, using his hands freely to illustrate whatever he was saying. So much for Otto being shy around women! Later Mom told me it was stories about clocks from the Black Forest in Germany. I couldn't imagine what was funny about that, but I didn't ask.

At dinner, talk turned to Tom Lattimore's proposed shopping center. This was the first that Buck had heard of it, and he was immediately angry. "We can't have that in this neighborhood. Mess up traffic something horrible, bring in outsiders, troublemakers."

"I can't imagine that troublemakers will shop at an upscale grocery," I said mildly.

But he glared at me and answered, "They'll be drawn to pick pockets, grab purses, even steal cars. It's a petty thief 'come and get it' signal."

I doubted it was that bad, but I was glad he was on our side.

Mom surprised me by asking, "What's the plan to stop it?"

"The neighborhood association will meet next week—you should get an announcement any day—and we'll need people to walk the neighborhood and get signatures on petitions."

"I'll do that," Mom said quickly.

"Miss Cynthia, you will only do that in daylight hours," Keisha said with an air of authority. "You ain't goin' out at night."

"Evenings are when some of my neighbors are home," Mom said. "They work all day."

"I'll go with you, Miss Cynthia," Otto volunteered. I guess he had picked up Keisha's name for Mom. "And I can walk Magnolia, or at least large parts of it. I know a lot of the merchants."

"If you walk with me, Otto, I'll go with you on Magnolia. We can even stop for lunch at some of the restaurants," Mom said, and Mike threw an I-told-you-so look at me.

"I'll walk some in the evenings," Keisha said. "I know a handsome officer who will keep me safe."

Buck jumped to his feet. "Hold on, he's got more to do than escort you around the neighborhood!"

Keisha sighed. "I know that. I'll just keep him on speed dial. I do that anyway."

Mom's Italian cream cake was the sensation of the evening, with everyone eating pieces far larger than they should have. I worried about the girls waking in the night with upset tummies, but there was no way I could stop them from eating the delicious concoction. I thought about talking to Mom about less rich desserts and then decided against it—she was doing what made her happy.

"Miss Cynthia," Keisha said, affecting her best slow drawl, "you are sinful. This cake is sinful. And I love it. How about you, José?"

He raised his fork in appreciation.

Otto made a courtly bow. "Miss Cynthia, it is better than Black Forest cake and I never thought I would say anything good about Italy. You have charmed me."

Mom smiled, almost a secretive smile, and "Thank you, Otto."

Everyone left early—tomorrow was a business day. But their parting words mostly had to do with petitions. I'd call Jim Price in the morning and find out if they were ready. I promised to get them to everyone as soon as possible.

Keisha and José had brought Otto or I'm sure he would have insisted on seeing Mom home. Instead, Buck Conroy asked me, "Want me to follow your mama home?"

"I can get home by myself," Mom said frostily.

"I'll follow anyway. Just wait till we get McKenzie loaded."

Mom stalked out the door and took off without waiting. I was standing in the front door and saw the green Nova across the street follow Mom without turning its lights on. Buck saw it too, and left Joanie and McKenzie standing on the curb as he raced after Bella's car.

He was back in minutes. "She didn't follow your mom. Saw me and turned off on back streets. At least she doesn't know where your mom lives...yet."

Mom, I thought, didn't need another criminally insane person in her life. Now I had a new worry. Bella knew all about the whole family. Sooner or later, she'd figure out where Mom lived.

Dejectedly I went back inside the house. Mike had been sitting in his chair and missed the entire scene, but he sensed my mood. When he asked what was wrong, I told him about Bella's aborted attempt to follow Mom.

"We're getting you that handgun and signing you up for the course," he said. "As for your mom, we can't quarantine her...and she doesn't have a garage, so her car is in plain sight. Maybe Keisha should move back in."

"I can't ask her, not with José in the picture."

"Maybe she could stay with Claire. That's a big house."

He was grasping at straws in an effort to be helpful, but I knew Mom would never do that.

"We can get her a monitor to wear at home, like we got you, and tell her if she feels threatened to push the button—better safe than sorry. I'll tell her about the green Nova and if she sees it tailing her, she's to go straight to the police substation. It seems to me that one vengeful girl is causing us to make complicated plans—and we don't even know if she's dangerous."

"Not a chance we can take. What if she changes cars?"

"Joe doesn't think she will. Part of her strategy is to get on our nerves. She's sort of playing chicken, showing us how close she can get without getting caught." I was tired of talking about it and went to get the girls ready for bed.

****

The next day, after I picked Mike up at noon, he and I had a quick lunch at Nonna Tata, splitting a bowl of spaghetti puttanesca, and then I took him back to the substation. I checked in briefly with Keisha.

"Don't know what this world's coming to," she muttered. "Just let me at that girl for ten minutes. She won't bother you anymore."

"You know you can't do that—whatever it is you have in mind, and I don't want to ask."

"I'm getting me a knife in case she comes bargin' in here some day. Don't need a permit for that, and I know how to use it."

I rolled my eyes. "I'm going to Mom's. I need to warn her, tell her some precautions to take, just in case."

"And scare that poor woman to death? I best move back in there."

"What about José?"

"Well, I wouldn't have to stay with Miss Cynthia every night."

"Let's see what happens."

Mom wasn't home. Frustrated I sat in her driveway for a bit, but I knew I couldn't stay. I'd checked carefully to see

118

that Bella wasn't following me, but she could always just cruise the neighborhood and see me there. I went back to the office. Bella felt more and more like an albatross around my neck.

Back at the office I began to fret about Mom, and I called every few minutes to see if she was back home. She wasn't.

"You going to wear that phone out?" Keisha asked.

"I'm worried about Mom."

"Kelly, she's a grown lady. She can take care of herself. She's got more spirit than you know lately. She ain't the same woman that moved down here a year ago."

That didn't comfort me.

Finally, on my eighth try, Mom answered, and I immediately demanded, "Where have you been?"

"Why, Kelly, what's the matter dear?"

"Well, I ...I was just looking for you."

"Anything important? Are the girls all right?"

"They're fine, Mom. Where were you?" This time my question was calmer.

"Well, you know, I have your grandmother's clock—the old-fashioned chime one she went to school by."

Did I know? When I was a kid it sat right outside my bedroom and chimed every fifteen minutes plus tolling out the hour—drove me crazy some nights.

"Well, I just thought that nice Mr. Martin might fix it for me, so I went by his shop. My goodness he has a lot of clocks in there. So interesting. He told me about some of them, who they'd belonged to, how old they were. I was just fascinated. Then he mentioned that he lived behind his shop and only had a hot plate, so of course I had to offer to cook for him tonight—why didn't you tell me that before, Kelly? I went to the grocery store and got steak and potatoes. He said he'd walk, but I'll pick him up."

"Mom, then you'll have to drive him back to his shop

late at night."

"It won't be that late, Kelly, and it doesn't bother me to drive at night."

It bothered me for her to drive at night, a whole lot. "Mom, I've got to talk to you. It's important."

"Kelly, dear, can't you wait until tomorrow? I have so much to do before I pick Otto up."

I hung up and repeated the conversation to Keisha, who laughed and laughed. I knew Mike would do the same thing. *Mom was a head taller than Otto, for Pete's sake! What was she thinking?*

****

That night Mike used his walker and made it to the backyard via the ramp in front—a first. He threw the ball for the girls and Gus. As he always did, Gus caught it most of the time, but it was wonderful to watch Mike and the girls playing together again. Wonderful that is until Maggie pitched it back to him, a bit wide. He reached for it, lost his balance and fell on his bad leg.

Maggie screamed, I screamed, Em began to cry, and Gus ran over to lick Mike's face.

"Shall I call 911?" I asked.

Mike's face was pale, and he bit his lip as though in pain, but he said, "No. Don't call anybody. Just let me be a minute and then see if you and the girls can get me upright again. That was a damn fool thing to do—on my part."

Maggie wailed, "It's all my fault. I forgot and threw the ball back to you."

As color began to creep back into his face, Mike said, "It's nobody's fault, Mag. It's just one of those things that happen. Now let's see if we can get me up. Kelly, move the walker close where I can get a hold of it. My arms are still strong, and I can help pull myself up."

I did, and I bit my lip in worry, but we got him to a sitting position, put his arms on the walker, and then I put my arms under his and pulled up. Maggie stood behind him and pushed on his back to be sure he didn't fall backward. Em simply wailed. But soon he was standing.

"Can you walk?"

"Give me a minute. That was work for all of us."

After a few nervous minutes—nervous on my part if not his—Mike took a tentative step, first on his good leg, then on the injured one. "A little sore, but I think it's okay."

"You're going to the doctor tomorrow," I said.

"No." Firm.

"Yes." Equally firm. "If you can issue orders about guns, I can issue orders about doctors."

While he said, "Let's wait until tomorrow morning and see," Em screamed, "Gun? Who's got a gun?"

"Mike," I said calmly, my fingers crossed for the white lie. "His service revolver, and it's hidden up high where you can't get to it."

"Ugh," Maggie said. "Who would want to?"

Chapter Eleven

I called Mike's orthopedic surgeon first thing the next morning—I'd already dropped Mike off at the substation and heard all his protests that he was fine. But I thought he was limping more on the bad leg. Of course I was expecting and looking for the worst.

The receptionist said the doctor would see him when he began afternoon patient hours at two o'clock and please come a little early. I called Mike, told him I'd pick him up at 12:15 for lunch—his choice of places. He chose the Grill, and I wasn't sorry. After all, it was meatloaf day.

"You're making way too much of this, Kelly. I took a little fall. It could happen to anybody."

"Anybody doesn't have a broken leg. Besides, your regular appointment is next week—it's been eight weeks. Maybe this will substitute for that." I stared at him. "Mike, I'll leave the room, but please be honest with the doctor. Don't try to bluff your way through. Tell him if, when, and where it hurts."

He hung his head, and I knew he'd been planning on bluffing.

I sat in the waiting room, trying to read emails on my iPhone but swinging one foot in impatience and checking my watch so often I was tempted to shake it to see if it was still working. After twenty minutes, a nurse stuck her head out the door and said, "Ms. O'Connell, the doctor would like you to join them."

When I entered, Mike looked dejected. I shook hands with Dr. McAdams and took the chair he offered.

"He's given himself a set-back," the doctor said. "We'll

have to send him for x-rays to make sure the pins didn't get out of place. I didn't realize he was back at work full time, and I'm ordering him to cut back to half days—maybe mornings, so he can do his exercises, walk, and sleep in the afternoon."

I glanced at Mike, who did not look in my direction.

"He also asked if he could drive, but the answer is not for a while. I think in general Mike has been pushing himself too hard. He tells me it's difficult to get comfortable at night, and he admits that there isn't a moment in the day or night that he's not aware of his injury…and his limitations."

I wanted to shout, "Good for you and your honesty, Mike," but I kept quiet.

"I'm giving him a new regimen to follow," Dr. McAdams said, handing Mike several sheets. "You both need to realize that it will be a year before we know for sure if this surgery was a success. Mike could end up with one leg an inch shorter than the other…"

I saw Mike shudder just a bit.

"…and he's got to be careful and slow in this recovery."

I nodded but said nothing. I wasn't going to be put in the position of mothering him or giving him an opportunity to ask, "Want to say I told you so?" He did neither of those things but there was a great silent gulf between us on the way home. I dropped him off and went back to the office after making sure he was inside the house.

Late that night, when we were settled in bed, Mike reached for me and began to stroke my breasts, my stomach and on down. A sharp intake of breath and then, "Mike, are you sure it's okay?"

"Yeah, it's the one big thing I asked the doctor about and he said as long as we were careful."

I crawled on top of him and began nibbling at his ear

lobe. I was praying the girls didn't wake up.

****

Halloween was a bust at our house but a great success at the YMCA from all reports. Keisha went over to Mom's and gave out treats. Mike and I stayed home, and I answered the door while he, honest to gosh, sat with his service revolver tucked down in the chair next to him.

"If something happens," he explained, "I can't jump up to rescue you. This is the most practical solution."

"Is it legal? Besides, Bella won't come trick or treating. Not her style."

There were a few young Hispanic boys that for all I remembered could be Bella's younger brothers. But I doubted it.

Maggie had finally relented and repeated her costume of last year as a homeless person, with black paint smeared on her face to look like dirt and her hair deliberately soiled with actual dirt, hanging in strings around her face under an old beret. She was such a pretty child that I began to wish some year she'd choose a costume that showed off her prettiness. Em of course looked like an angel in her pink tutu.

Theresa brought them home around eight, knowing full well Em's eight-thirty bedtime, and they were laughing and full of stories of all they'd done—bobbed for apples, eaten caramel apples, played pin the tail on the donkey, done a sack race. A big part of me was jealous not to be part of the fun, and once again in my mind I blamed Sonny Adams for his reckless driving and Bella Garza for stalking me. If none of that had happened, my life would be free and unfettered as it was before Mike's accident.

I pulled Theresa aside to ask if she sighted Bella's car but she shook her head.

Next morning, Keisha reported all was calm at Mom's house and Mom had really enjoyed handing out treats.

Keisha had gone by to get Otto Martin, and the three of them drank wine, ate Halloween candy, and laughed a lot.

A momentary sulk: everyone had such fun except me. *Can it, Kelly, you have Mike alive and almost whole. Be grateful.*

****

Keisha and I were showing a house to one of Claire's friends when Mike called my cell phone. I excused myself and left the client to Keisha's care when I went out on the porch.

"Sonny Adams was killed last night," he said without preamble.

"Bella," I breathed. "So she *is* more dangerous than we thought."

"Probably so. They can't find her—doesn't seem to be on the streets. You seen her today?"

"No. Not since Sunday when she started to follow Mom home." I hesitated because I didn't want to hear the answer to my next question. "Was he shot?" It was almost a hopeful question. Guns apparently weren't Bella's style, so if he was shot it wasn't her. After all, Sonny Adams apparently had several shady connections. His death could be completely unrelated to Rosalinda Garza.

"Stabbed. In the belly, with a kitchen knife."

More detail than I needed.

"Conroy got a search warrant for the Garza home, but I don't expect he'll find Bella. Watch out. There's always the chance that she's gone on a tear."

I thought I might be sick for a moment. "Poor Mrs. Garza," I finally muttered.

'That's one way to look at it. Poor Sonny is another way."

"I have less sympathy for him."

"It's not a case of black and white, Kelly. Sonny was no credit to the human race, but Mrs. Garza has raised some kids who aren't either. I'll see you at noon for lunch.

Be careful." And he hung up.

I pulled myself together and returned to my client, who was listening to Keisha rattle on about the potential of this two-story brick house and making notes at the same time on a redo—the second story was already an add-on, and I too saw ways that it could be improved. "My contractor," I said, "could walk through with you and make suggestions. He's pretty good. I keep him busy, though, so he couldn't do the work." Okay, I'd just promoted Anthony, but I thought it sounded rather grand.

The client, Jerry Southerland, waved her hand. "Oh, we have a contractor. This will be the fourth house we've redone in ten years."

Sounded like I'd made an easy sale.

As I drove her back to the office, I looked down every side street, kept checking the rearview mirror, and clenched the wheel so tightly, she asked, "Kelly, is everything all right?" Keisha had come in her own car and dashed back to the office a few minutes ahead of us to put on the coffeepot.

It would have been so easy to sob and fall apart and say, "No, it's not. Everything's a mess," but I just mumbled, "Fine. I just like to be careful, especially with a client in the car…never know when someone will shoot out of one of these side streets."

She didn't look completely convinced, and I realized that was a dumb way to try to sell the neighborhood. When I pulled up next to her car, she turned to me and asked, "You're sure this neighborhood is safe?"

I tried, probably unsuccessfully, to laugh it off. "Of course. I'm raising my children here. And ask Claire. The only problems we've had lately had nothing to do with the neighborhood itself."

"Yes, I remember reading about that serial killer. You were involved, weren't you?"

No sense saying, "I was almost a victim," so I just said, "I tried to help with the case. My husband is a police officer."

"No wonder you feel safe."

"You really needn't worry," I said. Then impulsively I added, "There's a neighborhood association meeting Thursday night to deal with a zoning issue. Why not come meet the people who make up the neighborhood?"

She considered for a moment. "I'll see if my husband is free. That's a great idea. Thanks."

I told her it would be seven o'clock in the Hemphill Presbyterian Church—that caused her a moment's hesitation, since Hemphill didn't enjoy the best reputation of any street on the South Side, but she only skipped a beat. "We'll be there…and if Jake can't go with me, I'll see if Claire will."

"I'm sure she's going," I said, making a mental note to call Claire that afternoon.

As soon as Jerry was out of the car, I sped off to the elementary school, my heart in my throat. I cruised slowly, all around—the parking lot, the street in front of the school and the playground. No green Nova, no brown Mustang. Bella must be hiding out.

Relieved, I went to get Mike and take him home for lunch.

We were both sort of silent beyond the usual, "How was your day?" but then Mike said, "Kelly, promise me something."

"What?" I could hardly eat my tuna fish sandwich.

"You won't go rushing up to the Garza house."

That was an easy one. "No, I won't. I know I'm the last person they want to see, and now I really am afraid of Bella."

"Good girl."

I left, with Mike's promise that he would nap and then

exercise. "Don't you need a nap too?" His look was an outright leer.

"If I napped with you, I wouldn't get any sleep and neither would you."

"But exercise?" he persisted.

"Nope. I have things to do at the office."

"Okay." He was resigned. "When Maggie's home, I'll go with her to walk Gus around the block—yes, ma'am, with my walker."

"Will that be safe?"

"I have my revolver, remember? And a whistle. I doubt Bella will mess with a cop, even a disabled one. Besides I think she's hiding out."

I kissed him and fled.

Back at the office, I called Joe Mendez on his cell phone. He hadn't left yet for the YMCA. When I told him the news, he said, "I'll go up there tomorrow. Miss Kelly, you stay away."

I told him I'd already promised Mike that.

"I didn't tell you, but I got the two younger boys into alternative school the end of last week. I'll see if they're still going after this. And I may buy Bella a beer, if she's there."

"I haven't seen her since Sunday night, but that doesn't mean much. Mike thinks she's gone into hiding."

"Nah, it doesn't mean nothing. I'll see if that oldest boy will talk to me. I'll call tomorrow night."

Keisha gave me a curious look, so I told her the whole story, to which she replied, "Live dangerous, die young. That's why Joe's lucky you did what you did for him."

"Getting kind of hard-hearted, aren't you?"

"José's rubbing off on me. I think officers see so much of this stuff. It surprises you and me, but they know more about the dark side of people than we ever will—or want to."

Keisha, the philosopher. It seemed to me these days

that I was surrounded by threats and crime and, well, as she said, the dark side of people. But we were probably only seeing the tip of that old iceberg. I almost rushed back to take up a vigil outside the school.

When I took the girls home, I told Maggie that Mike would walk with her, but she might have to walk slow. He was back on his walker for an indefinite period of time.

"Is it okay for him to walk around the block?"

"Doctor says exercise is good for him." She would never understand my secret smile.

****

The morning paper the next day had a small article that the stabbing victim found off Northeast Twenty-Eighth Street had been identified as Sonny Adams. Police were looking for a "person of interest" but there wasn't much else. I called Mike.

"Beat me to it. I was going to call you. A team went through the Garza house thoroughly, found a butcher knife with bloodstains and fingerprints. They printed the only family member home, the mom, which is an insult to her and stupid on their part. Now they've still got to find Bella and print her, plus print all the brothers. The two younger ones were in school, so they'll get them this afternoon. No telling where the older boy is."

I hung up wishing some wonderfully bright idea would come to me, but none did.

Joe called a little later with essentially the same report, but with more humanity in it. Mrs. Garza, he said, was frantic with worry about her two older children, hadn't seen them in days. Michael and Alex, the two younger boys, were staying in school and had started going to the Boys and Girls Club after school. They claimed they had no homework, but Joe told her not to believe that. She blessed him, said the younger boys were the hope of her life, and sent him away with homemade tamales that he was saving to share with Theresa.

"I'm not sure what you got me into the middle of, Miss Kelly, but the tamale part is good. And I feel okay about Michael and Alex. Where are the police on this?"

I told him about bloodstains and fingerprints and that it would be a while before the lab results were in, but I'd let him know.

****

The neighborhood association meeting the next night was noisy and crowded. There were almost as many people as there had been when the neighborhood was scared out of its wits by a serial killer. I noticed that Jerry Southerland was there, apparently with her husband, sitting next to Claire. I gave Claire a hug and welcomed Jerry, who introduced me to Jake.

"Looks like we're about to become part of your neighborhood," he said. "Jerry isn't happy unless she's redoing a house. I like to keep her busy."

Everything about him, from clothes to watch to haircut, spoke money, so I guessed he could afford for Jerry to redo old houses, but I resented his patronizing attitude—treating her as though she were the "little lady" to be kept amused.

I managed a smile. "We'll be glad to have you. I'm sure you'll like it."

When I came back to Mike, he said, "What's the tight little smile about?"

"Tell you later." I looked around and noticed that Tom Lattimore was conspicuously absent from the meeting.

Jim Price called the meeting to order and quickly outlined why we were there. Then he asked for those who wanted to speak to line up at a microphone in the center aisle. Christian was the first to speak, and he had the most important information. He had read the zoning variance application, which indicated, as far as his research could tell,

130

Tom Lattimore's investors were not from Fort Worth. Christian emphasized that meant that they were interested in money and not in our neighborhood. Then he reported that the petitions Lattimore had submitted contained 131 signatures, a fairly insignificant amount in a neighborhood the size of ours. About one-third of them proved to come from outside the official boundaries of the neighborhood.

When Christian sat down, Jim Price spoke to report that without an organized effort, the neighborhood association had 457 signatures. A door-to-door campaign was planned, and there would be petitions and volunteer sheets at the table in the back of the room at the end of the meeting.

Several neighborhood people spoke, among them Keisha, who repeated her plea for the neighborhood pretty much as she had given it in the office earlier. Otto Martin had been persuaded—perhaps with Mom's help—not to talk, partly because the idea of him living behind his store was iffy and mostly because no one wanted him threatening again to kill Tom Lattimore. He had walked to the meeting, since it wasn't far from his store, but he now sat next to Mom, which caused Mike to poke me in the ribs and grin knowingly.

The meeting went on predictably. No one spoke for the development plan until to my surprise and dismay Jake Southerland stood at the mike. "I'm not a resident of Fairmount," he began, "but my wife is trying to convince me to buy a house here to redo. After listening to this discussion tonight, I can tell you that I will never invest money in this neighborhood. I'm a businessman, a developer, and I make my living building new shopping facilities. Leaving old buildings untouched and saving mom-and-pop stores doesn't make money—building new big business that will draw customers does. You people need to wake up to the twenty-first century."

He sat down to stunned silence. Fairmount people were too polite to boo, but I sure was tempted. Mike simply squeezed my hand.

After an awkward silence, Jim asked if anyone else wanted to speak in favor of the development. Dead silence. So he covered a few other routine business matters—a treasury report, the selection of a couple of new block captains—Claire volunteered to my great delight, while Mike held my hand down tight to keep me from jumping up—and we needed a new monitor for the neighborhood e-newsletter. I grabbed my hand from Mike and raised my hand. When he frowned at me, I said, "Piece of cake. Not hard to do. Doesn't take a lot of time."

Mike shook his head.

We hurried home after the meeting, knowing we had kept Theresa and Joe out far past their usual bedtime. Instead of finding them pacing the floor anxious to go home, we found Bella's car parked in front of the house and Joe leaning in the driver's window talking to her. When she saw us turn into the driveway, she pulled away so fast that Joe was in serious danger of being dragged. Fortunately, he had good reflexes and jumped back in time.

He stood staring after the car for a minute then met us in the driveway. "Little bitch," he muttered. "Sorry, Miss Kelly. I apologize. But she nearly dragged me. Didn't give me no warning she was going to pull out like that."

"You okay?" Mike asked. "We can put out a warrant if she hurt you."

"Nah, I'm just mad. I went out to try to talk some sense into her, but I don't think she's the listening kind. Asked her why she was doing this to perfectly good people and she said, 'There ain't perfectly good people in this world.' So I told her oh yeah, there are and you two are them. I tell you one thing, she's not doubled over with grief. We talked about Rosalinda a bit. Bella didn't like her much. Rosalinda was the pretty one, the one who got good grades, the one who snagged a boyfriend with money—though I don't think Sonny Adams was much of a catch."

"So why kill Sonny Adams?" I asked. "And why stalk me?"

Mike looked startled. "She hasn't been charged. Neither has her brother."

"Partly because no one could find her. Tonight's the first time she's shown up since Adams was killed. She did it," I said and sailed into the house leaving the two of them on the sidewalk. Theresa was at the dining table, taking notes out of a textbook. "Hi, Miss Kelly. I don't think I'll ever understand economics. To me it's simple: you earn money, you pay your bills, and you put some in the bank. But that's sure not the way governments do it."

"So I've noticed," I said.

Theresa sighed and closed the book. "Girls were angels. Joe read to them so I could study, and they went right to sleep…in your bed, I'm afraid. Where's Joe? He said he was going out for fresh air. If he's out there smoking…."

"He and Mike are just chatting."

"I bet," she said suspiciously. "That girl still following you?"

"Yep. She was outside tonight. That's really why Joe went out."

Theresa sighed. "Puts himself in danger all the time for others. He's got a knife, but…."

Alarmed, I said, "He mustn't carry a knife, Theresa. It violates his probation."

"Some of his former buddies don't see it that way. They might jump him some night. We're both aware of that. He's not carrying a gun, at least."

I wasn't the only one living with fear.

Chapter Twelve

The next day when I picked Mike up from the substation at noon, he announced we were lunching at the Grill and then going gun shopping. I balked—I had work to do, I couldn't be out of the office that long, I had to pick up the girls.

"If you don't stop babbling, I'll drive the car. There's a good gun shop out on Old Highway 80."

"Is it a pawn shop?"

Large sigh. "No, Kelly. They sell guns, new and used. We'll get you a new one."

Right. I don't want a used one. Who knows whom it might have killed in its previous existence?

The shop was innocuous enough with a small sign saying, "Hank's Guns and Pistol Range."

Pistol range? Did I have to shoot the blasted thing today? I wasn't up to it. I needed time to prepare.

"Kelly, let me do the talking please."

I bristled. Mike knew I didn't like being treated like the female idiot in the crowd. I'm not even blonde for pity's sake.

He introduced me to Hank. I had expected big muscles, tough guy type, tattoos, maybe a cigarette hanging out of his mouth ala Humphrey Bogart. Instead a perfectly ordinary man, slightly on the small side, wearing spectacles and looking anything but threatening, shook my hand firmly and said how nice it was to meet me. I returned the greeting, sort of under my breath.

Mike explained I needed some protection, nothing big, something easy for my purse. A handgun, he said, not a semi-automatic.

Hank had just the thing. He disappeared and came back with a small box. Inside, wrapped in tissue like fine jewelry was a small gun, maybe the length of my hand. Hank put it in his palm and hefted it. "Nice weight. Not too heavy, not too lightweight. Here, try." And he gave it to Mike. "Smith & Wesson."

I wanted to scream, "Wait a minute! This is for me!"

Mike moved it around in his hand, juggled it to tell the weight, and said, "Here, Kelly. Just hold it."

I expected my hand to drop under the weight, but it didn't. The gun was light, maybe a pound. And I guess it was what I'd heard on detective shows as snub-nosed—the barrel (I assumed that was what it was) was short, just over an inch. But still, I held it awkwardly.

Mike took my hand, rearranged the gun so it lay in my palm, and then showed me how to turn my hand up and pull the trigger. "Don't pull it," he said. "You don't know if this gun is loaded or not."

Surely he trusted Hank not to hand me a loaded pistol. That would be disaster for everyone.

Hank nodded. "It's not loaded. I assure you of that. But you still have to check for yourself." He showed me how to open what I would later learn was the chamber and roll the cylinders to make sure all were empty.

Mike carefully positioned it in my hand and said, "Aim it. Not at Hank, even though you know it's empty. Never point a gun at a person unless you mean to shoot him or her." He showed me how to hold both hands straight out in front of me at chest level. "What are you aiming at?"

"That poster on the wall, the picture of the big game hunter." I hate big game hunters.

"You're probably going to be three feet to the right of it. That's why you need target practice. When are the concealed handgun license courses, Hank?"

"Every Saturday, nine o'clock."

"Sign her up. She'll be here, maybe next week if she's a quick learner."

I started to protest. How did he know I didn't have client appointments or classes for the girls or...that was it. "Maggie has a soccer game Saturday morning. Ten o'clock. And you can't drive."

"Keisha or Claire will take her. You'll be here if I have to come with you." He turned away from me. "Hank, okay if we go do a little target practice now?"

"Sure thing. Ear muffs are out there."

Mike showed me how to load the thing. The .38 caliber bullets were amazingly small—about as long as the first joint of my thumb and tiny around. "This can hurt someone?"

"This can kill someone," he said firmly. "That's why you take it very seriously. And you never shoot without meaning to kill. Don't aim for the legs or something like that because you might not stop the person. Besides the trunk of the body is the easiest target."

I can't do this. Yes, I can. I promised.

Mike wasn't through with his instructions and demonstrations. He told me to spread my legs until my feet were under my shoulders, bend my knees slightly, and use both hands on the gun, although I'd squeeze the trigger with my right index figure. It took me so long to figure out the pose that I'd have to ask any threatening opponent to please stand still for a moment while I assumed the stance.

"And, Kelly, keep your eyes open when you shoot. Don't shut them. Lots of women are tempted to do that."

It was all way too complicated. "What if I don't have time to remember all those instructions?"

"Just shoot," he said.

We put on earmuffs, and I found myself shooting at the outline of a man, with a bull's eye where his heart should be. Somehow that was a lot different than shooting at a real person, and after a few shots that went wild, then a few that hit other parts of the target, I got in a head shot and one close to the heart. Darn! I was good at this, and, to my dismay, I began to enjoy it. In fact, I used up all the ammunition Hank had sent us with—practice bullets, though I didn't know it at the time. It might have diminished my sense of achievement. Anyway, I was slightly disappointed when Mike called it quits.

"We'll practice every day this week," he said. "You should be ready for the class on Saturday."

"Every day?"

"Yep, every day."

"How'd she do?" Hank asked.

"Like a pro," Mike said. "She's going to be good."

I murmured something about beginner's luck and reminded myself that if I ever did have to shoot at a living person, it would be a lot different. I still didn't think I could do it. We paid an exorbitant amount for this small gun and left with barely time to get the girls. When they asked where we'd been, I said, "Mike and I did some shopping," and dared him, with a long look, to be more specific. The girls were not to know about our purchase.

****

Keisha asked about my afternoon the next morning and I told her the truth but emphasized I didn't want the girls to know about it. "Those girls figure out more than you know," she retorted. When I told her about my daylong session Saturday and Maggie's game, she immediately said she and José would take her. "José used to play soccer. He can give her some pointers."

I wasn't at all sure that was what Maggie would want.

Meanwhile, I told her I'd be at the range every afternoon, per Mike's orders, and she laughed.

Thanks for your support, Keisha.

Joe called to report he was off for the day and would be trying to catch up with Bella.

"The police haven't found her, Joe. I don't know how you can."

"She's not following you?"

"No, not since the other night. I don't know why she turned up outside our house last night, but I suspect she knows they found a bloody butcher knife at her mom's house and they want to fingerprint her and Ben."

"I bet I can find her," he said, and I decided there were some things it was better not to ask Joe about.

Sure enough he reported that night he'd found her and Ben, hiding out in an abandoned building, apparently one that several homeless kids stayed in. He wouldn't tell me more—"I can't betray a trust," he said. "She says she didn't kill Sonny and neither did Ben. She didn't much like him, but as she put it 'He wasn't worth killing—not over Rosalinda.'" He paused a minute and said, "She did tell me Rosalinda was pregnant. She hadn't told anyone yet except Bella. I gathered she kind of lorded it over Bella with how good Sonny was going to be to her and her child."

That led my mind on a whole different train of thought—perhaps Sonny had almost staged that accident so he could get rid of Rosalinda. Gruesome thought—and it made me angry all over again. To think Mike might have been killed because that scum—excuse me, don't talk ill of the dead—wanted to dump a pregnant girlfriend. Surely not. How could he be sure she'd be killed—or at least lose the baby—and he wouldn't be hurt? But back to Bella and Ben.

"If they're innocent, why don't they come forward and let themselves be fingerprinted?"

"If they're innocent, and it's a big if, they still don't trust police. Call them 'the man.' She asked me if I knew anything about a big development on Magnolia Avenue.

Told her I don't."

"I do, Joe. I'm opposed to it."

"She said Sonny Adams was mixed up in that and that's probably why he got killed."

How would she know that? And what did that have to do with her stalking me?

"If she didn't like Rosalinda or Sonny either one, why stalk me?"

"I haven't figured that out. I asked her, and that's when she looked scared, said she couldn't talk to me anymore."

We talked a bit more, neither of us getting anywhere, and then said good night. I was totally confused.

I tried to repeat the conversation to Mike, but as I did it made even less sense.

"The good thing, Kelly, is that you don't have to figure it out. It's police business."

How many times have I heard that before? "I don't have to figure it out, but I have to be prepared to shoot someone to protect myself, my girls, you? That's even more confusing. Of course I have to figure it out."

"Mom, you're not going to shoot anyone, are you?" Em had come quietly into the room and now stood in front of me, looking very solemn.

I swept her into my arms. "Of course not, darling. Mike and I were having a hypothetical conversation."

"What's hypo-et-ical?"

"Hypothetical," Maggie said calmly, coming up behind her sister. "It means it's not really going to happen."

"I don't want Mommy to shoot anyone."

Neither does Mommy, I thought.

I tossed and turned that night, and I know I disturbed Mike, who found it hard enough to find a comfortable position where his hip didn't hurt him. Finally I went into the living room and curled up on the couch. It wasn't as comfortable as curling up next to Mike.

I guess it was three in the morning when Mike, using his cane, came into the living room and sat on the edge of the couch.

"Can't sleep," I muttered into my pillow.

"Because you're trying too hard to figure all this out."

"And you're not?" I thought he should at least be as puzzled as I was. "Aren't you worried?"

"Yeah, I am. Mostly about you." He stroked my hair. "I'll talk it all out with Conroy tomorrow, though you know what he'll say about Joe being involved."

"Don't say anything about how or where Joe found Bella. I wish you didn't have to tell him about Joe at all. Joe doesn't want to be a snitch, and Theresa says there's always a chance someone will retaliate for his having gone over to, oh I don't know, the other side."

"What other side?" Mike was grinning. I could see his face in the reflection from the streetlight.

"The law-abiding side."

"I suppose he's right. I'll work it out with him to keep Joe out of it."

"And I'll call Tom Lattimore tomorrow, see if I can find anything out."

"Kelly, wait till next week to do that."

I sat up. "Why?"

"'Cause you'll have a gun then. Come on back to bed."

I overslept, the girls were late to school, Mike was late to his desk, and Keisha gave me a skeptical look.

****

Mike wasn't fooling. We went to the practice range every day for two hours or more. He made me take apart that gun, load it and reload it more times than I care to remember. He moved targets closer to me, than farther away. He narrowed the range of the target until I could put five out of five bullets within quite a small circle and at a fairly distant range. And I did it repeatedly. He beamed like a proud father.

Friday, as we left the range, he said, "I think you're ready. All those practices I made you do are what they'll ask you to do in the exam."

"Exam? I thought it was just…well, you know…they'd talk a lot and I'd sign my life away if I shot somebody and that was it."

"Nope. It's a test. You have to demonstrate that you can shoot."

Saturday wasn't nearly as long a day as I expected. The class began with lectures—about safety, about where you could and couldn't carry a concealed handgun. The State of Texas has a thick book of regulations—no way could I remember all of them, but I think I got the basics. There was a quiz, and apparently I passed, because Hank didn't pull me out of the class.

Hank showed some purses that had built-in sleeve-like things so you didn't have to dig in your purse to find your gun. "Excuse me, would you stand right there? Don't shoot me yet, because I'm still looking for my gun." Since I dig in my purse all the time for my keys, the purse wasn't a bad idea—but it was expensive, and I still didn't think I was ever going to use that gun. There were practice sessions on cleaning a gun, loading it, unloading it, etc. Over half the people in the class of about twelve looked to be thoroughly familiar with guns and fairly bored with this part. We also had to fill out endless forms about our background, occupation, all that stuff. I presume they do a background check on everyone who applies for a CHL.

Finally, after I ate my tuna sandwich from home with a Coke from the machine during a short lunch break, it was time for the range test. I wouldn't ever tell Mike that I looked forward to that part of the day. Once again I did well—in fact, I ended up at the head of the class, much to the disgust of some of the more seasoned shooters among us.

"Tell Mike you get a gold star for the day—and a permit." He handed me the permit. "Keep this on you at all times when you're carrying."

I almost asked carrying what, but I caught myself in time. Instead, I said, "Is that like the smiley face my girls get at school?"

Hank was taken aback, but he finally said, "Well, I guess so."

When I got home, Mike announced that the girls wanted pizza and we were going to Chadra. Claire and Liz would meet us, but Megan was busy—a date, he thought. Sounded good to me.

We had a happy dinner, with thoughts of guns and stalkers and Tom Lattimore far from my mind. The girls and Liz wanted pizza, while Claire and I settled for the restaurant's big salads and Mike ordered chicken schwarma.

Liz regaled us with tales of high school life, and Maggie hung on her every word. Em stared more skeptically when Liz talked about crushes on boys and who liked who.

"So is there someone special in your life, Liz?" Mike asked.

She as much as glared at her mother. "No, Mom won't let me date until I'm sixteen. Or drive."

Claire remained calm under the stare directed at her. "Soon enough, my dear, and then there will be rules. Ask Megan."

"Mom, that was a long time ago."

"Hmmm. Three years, I think."

"Well things are different now."

"They sure are. Your texting bill is out of sight."

Primly Liz said, "I can afford it," and I saw Claire clench her jaw. According to Jim Guthrie's will, Liz had a monthly allowance that was probably twice what a girl her age should have. And Megan got no money. Apparently all the tension between Claire and Liz wasn't resolved.

"I want a cell phone," Maggie said. "All my friends have iPhones."

Mike and I exchanged glances, and he spoke. "An iPhone is pretty expensive, but we might consider looking at some other smart phones. Isn't Christmas coming?"

"Do I have to wait that long?" Maggie wailed.

Liz jumped in. "Maggie, I didn't get one until I was in high school. My dad got it for me."

That little barb again. I decided it was time to change the subject.

"Thanksgiving is coming, and I don't think Mom wants to do it at her house. Too many painful memories of last year, when she was so happy that Ralphie joined us." Actually, Mom hadn't said that, but I suspected she wouldn't want to hostess and I'd present it to her tactfully.

"His name was Ralph," Em corrected. She didn't understand I couldn't think of him as anything other than Ralphie when he confessed how he'd hated it when his mother and her friends called him that well after he was grown.

"Uh, my mistake. Anyway, you all understand. Other than that, I think we'd want the same crowd, except Keisha will want to bring José and I suspect both Keisha and Mom will want Otto included."

Claire was behind times, and we had to explain about Keisha's new beau, José, and Mom's new friend—I thought the term beau wildly inappropriate—Otto. Claire laughed at the story of Keisha and Mom practically fighting to see which one could adopt Otto and feed him more often. Then she sobered. "My house was built for entertaining"— she shot a glance at me, for after all it had been my house before I sold it to her—"and I'd love to host this year."

"We'll all bring something," I said. "Let me make a list of who's coming and then we can find out what each one wants to provide."

"I insist on fixing the turkey," Claire said. "I saw some great recipes in the new *Bon Appétit.*"

Mike groaned. "Can't we just have plain old-fashioned turkey?"

"Hush." I squeezed his knee under the table. "You know what Claire fixes will be good."

"And you can carve, Mike," she added.

"Oh, great." But he smiled. His arm had been out of the cast for a while, and he could now carve with both arms. I think he was pleased to be asked.

"I can make onion soup dip," Maggie said proudly, and Em looked crestfallen until I assured her we'd find something for her to make.

"It's only two weeks away," I said. "We've got to get busy."

Late that night, when Mike plaintively asked, "Aren't you coming to bed?" I replied, "In a minute. I'm making a Thanksgiving list—it's really long, as I expected." And it was: Anthony and his sons, Theresa and Joe, Mike, me and the girls, Mom, Keisha and José and Keisha's mom, Claire and her girls. Oh, yes, and Otto. Why was he always an afterthought? "Sixteen of us."

"I didn't know we had that many friends," Mike said, and I nearly threw a legal pad at him. Then I turned out the light and climbed into bed, my thoughts full of how to spark up the traditional menu without abandoning it.

As he reached for me, Mike said, "I do not want to debate the various ways of cooking a turkey."

Chapter Thirteen

Monday morning in the office, I was worrying about how to approach Tom Lattimore. I hadn't forgotten Bella's words that the development held the secret to Sonny Adams' murder and the implication that Lattimore might hold the secrets to a lot more things. But I was not going to be a hypocrite and call to ask brightly how the plans for the presentation to the Historic Landmark Commission were going. I certainly wasn't going to gloat over the Zoning Commission's decision to delay their verdict. I hadn't talked to Tom since—and our last two lunches had ended disastrously—so I was drawing a blank on a pretense to call him. Unless I just called and asked bluntly what he knew about Sonny Adams. *Not a good idea, Kelly. Cancel.*

I'd shuffle papers, read a few new MLS listings, sit and stare, then shuffle papers again. Getting nowhere. Until the phone rang about ten, and Keisha said, "Certainly, Mr. Lattimore. I'll put you through."

"Put you through," meant "I'll hold my hand over the receiver and tell her it's you."

I answered as cheerfully as possible. "Hi, Tom, how's it going?"

"Fine, Kelly, just fine. But I wanted to apologize for a couple of things. One is that I did not put Jake Southerland up to what he said the other night."

"I know. His wife is a client of mine."

He coughed self-consciously. "Ah, not any more, Kelly. I just sold them a house in Berkeley. Sorry. But Jake didn't want to deal with you any more after that meeting."

This conversation wasn't going well, but I tried to tell

myself that in real estate, as in any other business, you win some and you lose some. So my reply was honest: "I'm sorry to lose a sale. I had a house that his wife really liked."

"Someone else will like it just as well. But, Kelly, we've been friends a long time, and I want to keep it that way. Our last two lunches were pretty, well…what's the word I want?"

This time I couldn't resist. "How about disastrous?"

That cough again. "Yes, they were disasters. I want to take you to lunch to make amends. We won't talk about developments. Just visit for old times' sake."

If Tom Lattimore thought he wasn't as transparent as a sheet of clean glass, he needed his brain examined. But it might be worth it to see what he wanted. And I could slip in my Sonny Adams question.

"Sounds good, Tom. Let's mend fences."

"Indeed. How about today or are you booked?"

Hmmm. I could pretend to have a busy schedule and fit lunch in a week from Thursday—or I could be honest and say today would be fine, which is what I did.

"Great. No tacos. No Chadra. How about meeting at Carshon's? I love that place, and I don't get there often enough."

Claire and I had been there recently, but I was game. "Sure, I can meet you there—say twelve thirty?"

"I'll be there," he promised.

I took Mike home at noon, made him a sandwich, pleaded an appointment and left. He was preoccupied with a cold case file someone had thrown on his desk this morning and barely noticed that I wasn't eating lunch with him.

"Sure, hon. See you tonight."

Tom Lattimore had secured a table in a remote corner of Carshon's. "It's rarely quiet here," he said, rising to greet me. "But this is the best I could do, and besides, we aren't telling secrets, are we?" He grinned conspiratorially, making me his ally—or so he thought.

"My treat. What will you have? I recommend the Reuben."

I love Carshon's Reuben sandwiches and was sorely tempted. But I resisted and ordered lox and cream cheese but with rye toast instead of a bagel. Tom gave me a strange look but ordered a grilled Reuben with pastrami. "Kelly, I got you here under false pretenses. I want your help." His smile was his most charming and disarming.

I was neither charmed nor disarmed. "How so?"

"It looks like the development is going down the tubes, and my backers want me to do whatever I can to pull it out. So I want your advice."

"Move it to Eighth Avenue," I said bluntly, spreading cream cheese on my toast.

He took a bite of his Reuben and chewed thoughtfully. "There's not a perfect space there."

"Neither is there on Magnolia."

"Kelly, what would make it acceptable to you?"

I thought seriously about his question. "My big objection is disrupting the small businesses currently in that strip of historic buildings. That's a biggie, and I don't see a way around it."

"What else?" he prodded.

"Off-street parking. I guess, if you could find a non-historic site and put the parking behind the store it would help a lot. Then dispense with the auxiliary stores. Just the one big store." I thought I should toss him a bone. "It does sound like someplace I'd like to shop."

"I knew you'd see it my way.'

Well, not exactly.

"What's your best advice, Kelly? I'm serious. I need help here."

"Find another location. How about Hemphill? There

must be a lot of property there that you could buy reasonably and tear down with a clear conscience."

He scoffed. "Hemphill is the other side of the tracks as far as people in Berkeley, let alone Fairmount, are concerned."

"There's not much on Rosedale."

"Out of my target area."

"And no side streets in Fairmount would allow it. I don't know, Tom. I'm back to Eighth Avenue. It seems to me your best bet. I saw a vacant lot next to Pendery's Spices, but I suppose it's not big enough."

He shook his head.

"Who owns that property on the north side of Windsor just across the tracks from Eighth?"

"No idea. I guess I could investigate. But here's an idea: how about if I got all the tenants of the historic buildings to agree to sell their businesses and renovated those buildings into one huge store, with parking in the rear?"

"John Henry Jackson already told me about that plan. It might just work, but I don't think those tenants want to move. And I own two of the buildings. I won't sell easily."

"I understand, but I can explore possibilities there. Oh, and the property on Eighth. You've given me some good ideas, and I'm indebted enough to buy you chocolate pie."

I laughed and said no, but I'd sit while he ate a piece. I still hadn't gotten to my question. Tom ordered pie, and while we waited I said, "Tom, did you know someone named Sonny Adams?"

He thought for a long minute...or appeared to... then shook his head. "No, doesn't sound familiar. Why?"

"I heard by the grapevine that his death was related to the development plans on Magnolia."

"And you're interested *why?*"

"He was driving the car that hit Mike's patrol car."

"And he's dead now?"

"Yes. Apparently knifed on the North Side. He was a small-time criminal and that's pretty much where he operated."

"North Side? I own quite a bit of small rental property up there and hire people to collect rent for me. I don't recall the name but I can ask my accountant—he handles all that for me."

Slumlord! That proverbial light bulb went off in my head, but I said, oh so casually, "Would you ask and let me know what you find out?"

"Sure thing," he said, taking a bite of chocolate meringue pie that looked beyond tempting. "They brought two forks. Sure you don't want a bite?"

I was sure. I didn't want to seem so intimate with him.

We parted cordially, at least on the surface, but I felt tension between us. I was sure he knew more about Sonny Adams than he let on, and I knew in a day or so I'd get a phone call saying, "No, my accountant says he never hired anyone by that name." I also knew he wouldn't investigate that property for sale on Eighth Avenue. He knew I didn't trust him. We were at a Mexican standoff.

What I needed now, of all things, was Bella. And I hadn't seen her car in days. Just when I wanted to be stalked, my threatening shadow disappeared. I made one of my infamous spur-of-the-moment decisions, jumped in the car, and got out my cell phone.

"Keisha, I won't be in the office this afternoon. Going to do some field work."

"Why do I have the feeling I should go with you?"

"Don't be silly. Just checkin' out a few things."

"Uh huh, sure you are."

I headed for the Garza house. If I thought Joe was off, I'd have taken him, but Joe was increasingly uncomfortable about doing things behind Mike's back. I guess I was more used to it. Mike would have a fit if he knew, but he'd never know. I'd be back in time to get the girls as usual.

Mrs. Garza greeted me warily, but she opened the door. I looked around more carefully than I had last time. Inside, the house gave the same appearance as it did outside—a house someone had begun to redo and then suddenly stopped. The living room had worn bare floors, but there were strips of carpet tacking around the edges— someone had pulled up carpet, perhaps with the intention of redoing the floor or laying new carpet. The walls were freshly painted off-white, but the blinds were still old and crooked, the furniture worn and dirty.

We exchanged pleasantries. Well, at least I did. I asked about the younger boys, Michael and Alex, and she allowed herself a slight smile.

"They're good boys. That Joe, I owe him the world. He's got them back in school and going to that club where they play basketball and stuff. Evenings now, they mostly stay home and do their homework. I think it's better with Ben and Bella gone. I…I don't speak bad about any of my children, but those two, they're not a good influence…."

I started to cough uncontrollably (and deliberately) while she watched and finally made an attempt to pat me on the back. "You all right, Miss?"

Finally I squawked, "Water. Could I have a drink?"

Without a word she turned, presumably to the kitchen, and I followed. As I suspected, some of the appliances were old—the stove and the dishwasher, which apparently didn't work at all because dishes were stacked in a draining basket. But the refrigerator was new and a shiny microwave sat on one worn counter.

I took a healthy drink of, ugh, lukewarm water, cleared my throat, and apologized. "I don't know what got into me. Thank you so much." Another sip. "You were saying about Bella and Ben…they're not here?"

"No. They come by some but they don't stay here."

I sent silent thanks to Joe for opening up Mrs. Garza's mouth. Compared to last time, she was positively chatty, and I could only think she trusted me, at least a little bit, because of Joe's work with the younger boys.

"Mrs. Garza, do you rent this house?"

She nodded.

"Who is your landlord?"

"You mean who owns it? I don't know." A negative shake of the head. "I pay rent to some company."

"What company?"

She shuffled through some papers in one kitchen drawer and came up with a receipt that she showed me. She was paying $400 a month for what appeared to be a two-bedroom, ramshackle house. The receipt came from something called North Side Properties.

I thanked her and returned the receipt. "Do you mail them a check?"

"No. Someone comes by to collect each month, first day, prompt. I don't dare be late." Then she offered a surprising fact. "That's how Rosalinda met that Sonny Adams who killed her. He came by collecting rent."

Something flickered in the back of my mind. "Did he start to fix up the house? Buy new appliances, that sort of thing?"

"Yeah, until that accident. Then we didn't see him no more. Someone else came to collect the rent."

The front door opened and banged shut. A too-familiar voice called, "Ma? Where are you?"

I suspected Mrs. Garza spent most of her time in the front room in front of the TV and that's where Bella expected to find her. The look the older woman gave me was one of panic. She was afraid of her daughter!

"In the kitchen. With company." The last two words were meant to warn Bella away, but they didn't. She came striding into the kitchen, looking as fierce as before.

"I saw her car." To me, "What are you doing here, Ms. O'Connell? Leave my ma alone. She don't need you pestering her."

"Hello, Bella. Are you all right? I haven't seen you following me lately."

She looked directly at me. "I been busy. I got other responsibilities. Me and Ben, we got us a tiny apartment. Did you send that Joe fella after me? You know the cops found me soon after? They fingerprinted us but the prints didn't match the knife they found here. We're innocent, like I told that guy." She paused for dramatic effect and then said menacingly, "Maybe they should fingerprint Ma."

"Ma" looked terrified, even though they had already fingerprinted her.

Bella softened a bit. "Just joking, Ma. We know you wouldn't hurt anyone. That's what's wrong with you."

Talk about a dysfunctional parent/child relationship!

"I didn't know that. I'm glad you're not under suspicion. I'm also glad if you're not following me anymore." Did her comment mean someone hired her to follow me, as a paid responsibility?

"Don't let your guard down." She seemed to enjoy making me squirm, though I tried not to show my concern.

I had no answer, so I simply said, "I'll be leaving. Mrs. Garza, thanks for the visit. I hope Michael and Alex continue to do well. Bella, see you around." And I headed for the front room trying not to hurry and half expecting a knife in the back. On the way I passed two bedrooms, one on each side of the hall. One of them appeared completely redone and quite feminine. I couldn't imagine Bella in it.

The clock in the car told me I just had time to get the girls. I took off, too fast, and made it almost downtown on Henderson before I realized the car was getting harder and harder to steer. I had a flat tire—and I suspected from the slow leak that someone had loosened the cap on the air valve. I had never changed a tire in my life, and I was stuck in the midst of the Henderson Street Bridge. Pushing the hazard light button, I took out my phone and called Keisha.

"Got a flat. Will you go get the girls? Tell Mike I'll call Triple A and be there as soon as I can."

"Where are you?"

"Ryan Place," I lied.

"Okay, where are you really?"

My voice was weak. "In the damn middle of the Henderson Street Bridge."

"You been up to the North Side to see the Garzas," she said. It was a statement not a question.

"And boy, do I have a lot to tell."

"Me and Mike will be waiting."

"Keisha...."

"All right, all right. I'm going. And I'll keep my mouth shut. This better be good."

As I dialed Triple A, I saw the familiar flashing lights behind me. My heart sank—now word about my whereabouts would surely get back to Mike. At least I'd have a chance to confess all before I took him to the substation tomorrow.

The officer was not someone I knew. Young, very young, and polite, he said, "Looks like you need help, ma'am."

"I guess so. I'm dialing Triple A right now."

"Easier and quicker if I change it for you. Won't tie up traffic as long. You sure picked a dilly of a spot."

I nodded. "Actually, I think someone loosened the cap on the air valve so I had a slow leak. I've come three or four miles."

He nodded, escorted me to the back seat of his car, and asked for my keys. "You do have a spare?"

"One of those donut things."

Without a word, he got out his jack, my spare, and changed the tire efficiently and quickly. He barely looked dirty, but I offered him one of the wipes I carry for the girls, and he took it.

"Thanks very much." I hopped back in the car.

"Whoa," he said. "I have to fill out an incident report." He went to his car, reached in and came back with some paperwork on a clipboard. "Name?"

He was "just the facts, ma'am" polite and businesslike, but by the time he dismissed me, he knew everything about me, including the name of my nearest of kin—Officer Mike Shandy.

I concocted a story on my way home, but I might as well have saved my breath. Conroy beat me to it. Keisha was gone, and Mike was sitting in the dark in the living room. "Where are the girls?" I asked as lightly as I could, bending to give him a kiss.

He turned away from me. "They're in their rooms doing homework. I told them to stay there until I called them."

"Oh."

Strained silence, until he asked in a tightly controlled voice, "Do you have something to tell me?"

Mistakenly I decided offense was my best defense. "Why didn't you tell me Bella and Ben had been fingerprinted and cleared in Sonny Adams' death?"

"Because it's police business, not yours. It has nothing to do with real estate."

"Oh, but you're wrong. What I found out today is that Tom Lattimore's a slumlord, probably owns a company called North Side Properties, and Sonny Adams used to collect rent for him. That's how he met Rosalinda Garza. And my hunch is that Sonny was skimming off the top of the rents he collected—he started to redo the Garza's house, then quit when Rosalinda was killed. Bella told Joe the key to Sonny's murder had to do with the development on Magnolia."

Mike settled back on the couch. "I have a feeling you better start at the beginning and tell me the whole story."

"Want a beer first?" I asked stalling and wishing for a glass of wine.

"Not now. Talk."

And so I did. I told him the whole story, leaving nothing out. It took a long time, and he was speechless for a minute. Then, "Kelly, did you have your gun with you?"

"Yes," I said triumphantly, "In my jacket pocket."

"Were you wearing the jacket? It's been fairly warm today."

"No. It was in the car."

"I wish I could ground you like I can the girls," he said. "There's no sense going over all the reasons you shouldn't have done this. We've had that discussion, and it apparently does no good." He got up and stalked from the room, as much as a man using a walker can stalk.

I heard him tell the girls they could go see their mother if they wished. He slammed the bedroom door behind him—great, how was I supposed to change clothes? I remembered the one other time before we married that I truly angered him and didn't hear from him for four days. Then I'd wooed him back by inviting him to cook at a barbecue. I could hardly do that again.

And another thing bothered me. I wanted us to share parenting, but he'd taken to ordering the girls around without consulting me. Who was he to say when the girls could and could not see me? I'd attributed this to his post-stress crankiness, but it was something we'd have to work on—together.

"Mom?" Maggie voice was tentative. "What's the matter with Mike? Did we do something wrong?"

"No, girls." I gathered them into my arms. "I did."

"I'm sure you didn't mean to," Em said righteously.

Oh, but I did.

Dinner that night was silent and awkward and not very special—creamed tuna on toast. Mike and I both picked at our plates, and the girls, glancing nervously from one to the other, did the same. Finally Maggie said, "I'll help you with the dishes, Mom," and began to clear the table.

Mike sequestered himself in the bedroom again. *If he's going to hide in what was once my space, where am I going to spend the evening?* Without saying a word, I went into the bedroom, got a big T-shirt and sweat pants and the book I was reading.

The girls went willingly to bed, glad to escape in sleep the tension of the house, and I spent the evening sitting on the couch, unable to focus on the book in my lap. A few tears escaped and ran down my cheeks. I knew I had not brought about the end of the marriage—Mike and I would make up and get back on our old footing, but maybe not quite the same. Some shifting was inevitable. We were learning and growing together, but Lord, how it hurt.

He and his walker clumped out about ten-thirty. "You coming to bed?"

"I thought maybe I'd sleep on the couch."

"One thing I remember my dad saying is not to go to sleep angry with each other—and he and Mom were pretty solid for the fifty-plus years of their marriage. I don't want to go to bed angry."

"Can you let go of it?"

"I guess I'll have to, Kelly, because I know there's no changing you. No," he held up his hand in a "Stop" position. "Don't tell me how important it was or why you had to go up there today or even send Joe earlier. I'll rehash all that in time. But I want you to know one thing."

"Will it help if I promise never to do anything like that again?"

"No, because you'd only break your promise. I want you to know that I love you too much to let you take such risks. It scares me breathless. I know you couldn't take me with you—I'm no use these days, and I'm a police officer so I can't compromise myself on your wild errands. And I know I'd have forbidden it if you told me, so I sort of understand why you didn't."

I didn't tell him I was too old to be forbidden to do anything I wanted.

"But, Kelly, I hate it when you take chances." He finally sat down next to me and took my hand.

"And I hated it every night when you went out on patrol because I never knew when would be "the" night. The night of your accident one of my thoughts was, 'Okay, it's finally happened.' I knew it would."

"You married me knowing how I earned a living."

"And you married me knowing my tendency to follow my instincts and my curiosity."

"Touché. Couldn't you have thrown a bit of caution in with it?"

"I'll try," I said, reaching up to kiss him. It turned into a long passionate kiss, and I swear as we got up and headed for the bedroom, I saw Maggie streak for her own room. Mike and I grinned at each other and went to bed.

****

By Thanksgiving, Mike and I had made our peace. He had said there was nothing concrete in all that I found out, nothing he could turn in as solid evidence. I had checked out North Side Properties on the internet, MLS listings, and the phone book—and come up with only a post office box number and a phone number. When I called, I got an answering service. I asked if Sonny Adams had ever worked for the company, and a bored woman, cracking her gum, said she didn't know but would have someone call me. I doubted that would happen.

To my surprise, Tom called a few days later. "Kelly, about Sonny Adams. We had to let him go. He was skimming off the top of the rents."

When I thanked him, I said I had another question. "Who owns North Side Properties?

"I told you. It's my investment company."

When I told Mike about it, he said, "Kelly, you go from suspicion to conviction in one big leap. It doesn't work that way."

We put it all behind us for the holiday.

Claire's house had indeed been remodeled for entertaining by my ex-husband Tim who considered it a showcase for real estate in the area. A huge state-of-the-art kitchen, now several years old, still offered the latest in appliances and conveniences. It was a large, spacious room, easy to gather in. The girls perched comfortably on stools at the island, seats they remembered from childhood. And we gathered in the kitchen for wine—Claire had gotten sparkling cider for the girls and Anthony's sons. The dining area in the house was simply one end of the living room. Claire's long table sat ten, and Mike brought our folding table, which easily seated the overflow. The girls insisted on seats at the picnic table with Anthony's sons, Megan and Liz. The rest of the "grown-ups" sat at Claire's table, although I suspect Joe and Theresa were surprised at being considered adults. Claire had fixed a cider-glazed turkey with lager gravy she found in a magazine somewhere—not *Bon Appétit,* she claimed—and a lemony-mushroom stuffing, along with a side dish of roasted Brussels sprouts. Keisha brought sweet potato pie and her mom brought chocolate meringue and apple. My mom brought our family cranberry relish—the raw kind with apples and oranges all ground up—and Otto, who managed to find the seat next to Mom, raved about it. Anthony contributed a couple of good bottles of chardonnay, and we all had a feast.

The kids liked being at their own table because no one said brightly to them, "So, how's school?" At the adult table, talk started with politics—we turned out to be mostly liberals except for Otto who, oddly enough, supported big business. I thought Otto would be for the little guy. Maybe it was an Old World notion he brought from his past. From politics, we moved on to the threatened development on Magnolia but Otto looked almost apoplectic, and I changed the subject to a discussion of the new restaurants springing up in the neighborhood. Ellerbe had recently been chosen as one of the top ten new restaurants in the nation by *Bon Appétit*—no small feat. Magnolia Avenue was fast becoming the place to go. Our neighborhood was on the upswing.

Cleanup went fairly easily with everyone helping, including Anthony's sons, Stefan and Emil, and the girls, who cleared the table. Claire loaded the dishwasher, Mike washed, and I perched on a stool to dry the serving pieces. Claire, of course, owned several lovely sterling dishes.

Before we were through, Brandon Waggoner arrived from his family dinner to pick Megan up for a late date. He met with a formidable welcoming committee but handled himself well in such a situation, shaking hands, talking easily with kids and adults alike. He and Megan left amidst a shower of "Have fun" and "Be careful."

"Every time she leaves, I say a small prayer," Claire said to me. "I've discovered how fragile happiness can be."

I hugged her. We'd both learned a lot in the last couple of years.

After many thanks and exclamations of appreciation, we all began to leave. I think Mom was a bit put out that Keisha and José took Otto home, but Otto bowed gallantly over her hand and said, "I'll look forward to our next meeting." I got the feeling the time and place of that meeting was already set and wondered if it was time for a talk with Mom.

Later, Mike said, "Kelly, you're not her parent. You can't quiz her about a relationship with a man."

Well, darn, maybe she'll tell me on her own.

We were cuddled comfortably on the couch, reliving the evening, talking about how nice it was to have everyone together.

Quietly, Mike asked, "Did you see the green Nova pull away when we left Claire's? Bella's not gone...or maybe it was Ben. Kelly, be oh so careful."

His news put a big black cloud over what had been a lovely evening. I pulled closer to him and said, "I will."

I'd put Bella and Tom Lattimore out of my mind and now it seemed as if their shadows were sitting in the room with us.

Chapter Fourteen

Mom called early the next morning, her voice so high-pitched and hysterical I could hardly understand her. My first thought, of course, was that Bella threatened her. "Mom, slow down. Are you all right?"

"Yes," she yelled, "but Otto has been beaten."

"Beaten?" I know I sounded like a dummy. "Who beat him?"

"I don't know!"

I stifled the urge to tell her to use her inside voice. She was screaming at me, and I could tell she was crying.

"Mom, slow down, and tell me the whole story. No, wait. I'm giving the phone to Mike. I'll go to the other phone."

I handed Mike the bedroom phone and set off to locate the living room remote, wherever it might be. Fortunately, I found it on the coffee table. When I picked it up, Mike was speaking in comforting tones.

"Nana, tell me slowly how you know about this. Take a deep breath."

He was so good. I could hear her breathe, and her tone was lower when she came back on. "Otto called me about three this morning. When Keisha dropped him off, he went inside and found his store had been trashed. Clocks thrown around—no telling the damage. He says he stormed and threatened and began to try to right things. But about midnight, two men forced their way in his back door. Yes, he had it locked, but I suppose it wasn't very strong or secure."

"Did he say what they looked like, how they spoke?"

"They had Halloween masks on and didn't say much, except to warn him to sell his store. They beat him with a pistol—what do you call that?"

"Pistol-whipped," Mike supplied.

"Yes, that's what the police told him. Then they knocked him down, kicked him in the ribs and head, and left, with a threat to remember what they told him."

"He called the police?" Mike asked.

Mom took a deep breath. "Yes, and they took him to JPS and had him checked. He's got a bandaged broken rib, a badly bruised arm, and his face is a mess."

"Mom," I asked, "where are you?"

"With Otto. He called from the hospital, and I went to get him."

Swell. My mother was at JPS in the wee hours of the morning, when I'd have been terrified to go there.

"I went out and got him some breakfast this morning, but I think I'll take him home with me for a couple days, so I can feed him some proper food and see that he heals. Kelly, I know that sounds improper, but believe me, it's not. Otto and I are great companions…but he could never take your father's place. I'm over that now."

I breathed a sigh of relief, though this was no time for relief. "Whatever you say, Mom. I trust your judgment." Okay, my fingers were crossed.

"What about the store?" Mike asked.

"The police boarded up the back door, but it's still a mess. Otto can't begin to clean it up now. And he shouldn't. That's the least important thing."

"The most important," Mike said, "is to find out who did this and why. It may be Monday before I can work on that, this being a holiday. I'll call Conroy though."

"Thanks," Mom said. "I don't know what I expect you all to do, but I just had to tell you."

"Of course, Mom. I'd have been upset if you didn't.

Keep us posted."

"I guess I'll make a casserole," I said to Mike after we hung up.

"Hold on, Kelly. I think your mom really wants to do the cooking here. I have an idea, though I won't be much help."

I listened to him and began calling—Joe and Theresa, Anthony, Claire, Keisha. We formed a work crew. We would start right after lunch and optimistically thought we could clean up the shop by suppertime.

Mike and I took the girls and went to Mom's to check on Otto, tell him how sorry we were, and get the key to his store. We were there longer than I expected.

Otto was a mess, to put it bluntly. A black eye, bruises and scratches on his face, forehead and arms. We couldn't see the bandaged rib, of course, but I could tell from the way he held himself that he was in pain.

Mom, on the other hand, was in her element. She had propped Otto up in an easy chair, his feet on the hassock, an afghan covering his legs, a cup of tea—a real china cup, not a mug—beside him.

"Your mother, she treats me like an invalid." He gave Mom a fond smile.

Platonic? I wouldn't bet on it.

"I told her," he said, "I have to be up and clean my store. It will have to be closed today, but I want to open as usual Monday. Show them I am not afraid."

When I told him our cleaning plan, he was reluctant. "I appreciate it," he said. "But you would not know which parts go with which clocks. I can sort it out later."

I assured him we would carefully label small parts and put them with the clock by which we found them, as best we could. It wouldn't be foolproof, but we'd try. "It would take you weeks to clean this up. We can do it in a day."

He clasped his hand to his head and then winced—

he'd hit a bruise. "Ouch, you're right. I am so grateful. I will treat you all to dinner at In and Out."

I smiled. "No need, Otto. We care about you and we're glad to do this."

We assembled at the store's back door just after one o'clock. The front, with broken windows, was boarded up—Mike said the police probably did that. Anthony excused himself from the general clean up and started measuring the windows for repair. "Need a new front door. I'll go to Old Home Supply after I measure." He phoned the glass company with measurements for the front windows and set off to get a door.

The rest of the store at first glance was a hopeless mess. Wonderful antique clocks were thrown on the floor, swept off the counter, smashed. I didn't see how any could be saved, but that would be Otto's decision. He knew what to do. I didn't. All I knew was to begin to clean. We picked up all the large parts we could find, keeping clusters together. Since Mike couldn't clean, he labeled. Otto had a huge supply of those brown envelopes that are half-letter size, and we put what seemed to be related parts into an envelope and used masking tape to attach the envelope to the clock to which they seemed to belong. We made mistakes, I'm sure.

Mike also carefully pulled broken glass out of clock faces and put it in brown paper sacks we'd brought. We'd wrap it in layers of newspaper before putting it in a trash bag then in a recycling cart—didn't want sanitary employees hurt doing their job.

Sitting for a long time was hard for Mike, even with the pillow he carried at all times. Just as at the substation, he got up to walk around, but each time he did we all yelled at him to avoid glass here and watch where he was stepping there, until he muttered, "You'd think I was a clumsy ox."

I just looked at him. He knew he wasn't the world's

most graceful or best-balanced person these days.

We swept—and swept—and swept some more. Keisha and Theresa took over cleaning the shelves that lined the small shop, using damp paper towels to get the tiny fragments of glass. Claire worked on straightening Otto's living quarters, where the devastation was not as bad but still had to be put to order. She and her girls righted furniture, tsked over the couch that had been attacked with a knife.

"Tomorrow," Claire announced, "I'm doing the garage sale routine and refurbishing these rooms."

Otto's bed hadn't been savaged, so Claire stripped the bed clothing and put it aside to wash at home. She straightened and washed his few dishes—just in case, she said—and held up a bent hot plate in disgust. "Another item for my garage sale adventure. He needs a toaster oven too." Clearly, Claire was planning on setting Otto up for a long-term stay in these quarters.

With everyone working efficiently, I left to walk the block and check on the other tenants. Tanya was horrified and a bit scared.

"Someone came to see me, but he was polite and just talked. Offered me a lot of money and help in finding a new location. I said I'd think about it."

I pushed the quizzing further and found she was describing Tom Lattimore. Maybe his technique was to try the "I'll buy you out" approach first and get rough if the person refused, as Otto had done. Well, Otto had carried it one step beyond—he threatened.

The sushi restaurant was not yet open though I thought by three o'clock someone surely must be there. My pounding on the door brought a man in a toque who said he didn't know anything about it and I'd have to talk to the owner. When I asked who that was and where I could find him, he shrugged and said to come back for supper. A quick look at the menu in the window—and the prices—convinced me I wouldn't be doing that.

I got sort of the same non-response all along the street—the taqueria owner said he didn't want trouble and it wasn't worth it to him to stay if somebody threatened to trash his equipment and beat him up. He was nervous, and I could tell he was making plans to move on. Taquerias are apparently fairly portable.

As I walked back to Otto's shop, I was close to exploding with anger. How could Tom Lattimore threaten people, even send goons to destroy property and beat the shop owner? I definitely felt a confrontation with him coming on.

By the end of that day, Anthony had installed a new door—I asked for the bill from Old Home Supply—and said the glass people would install the windows the next day. The shop was in as good an order as it could be until Otto had a chance to work on it. Some of the clocks were beyond repair—we all knew that. Some, Anthony said, could be fixed with the right wood—he seemed anxious to be able to use his fine woodworking skills, a contrast to his daily carpentry. I didn't really have a project for him now, so I would be glad if he found another outlet for his energy and skills.

We called it a day about six and most of us trooped to the Grill for supper. Em announced, "Work is hard, and I'm tired. I need pancakes." The Grill serves wonderful pancakes for breakfast but not at supper. Still, Peter accommodated her request, and she got her short stack, with bacon. I had the new Caesar salad with scallops and loved it.

We were home in bed by nine, though I did call Mom and tell her we would take Otto back to his place on Sunday. By then we hoped to have it stocked with food, livable, and the shop part in the best shape we could get it.

"Oh, Kelly, I wanted to take Otto to church Sunday morning. He's not much of a churchgoer—raised Catholic and all—but he said he'd go."

"Does he have church clothes?" I asked.

Her reply was sanctimonious. "The Lord does not care what you wear to church on Sundays. It's your soul he's concerned about."

My mother always cared how I looked on Sunday morning, ever since I could remember. What had happened to Cynthia O'Connell?

By Saturday late afternoon, Otto's shop was a new place—in fact, so new I was afraid he wouldn't like it. His living quarters were much warmer and more welcoming, less like a collection of Goodwill furniture. Claire had put in a brightly striped loveseat featuring brown and turquoise and a turquoise overstuffed chair with matching ottoman and throw pillows of beige, brown and gold thrown about. A small coffee table held Otto's collection of clock magazines, and a bookshelf mounted on the wall held his treasured book collection, which the vandals had not touched—probably they weren't readers and didn't realize how valuable those were to Otto. Claire completed the renovation with a small end table and a tasteful table lamp, eliminating the need for what had long been a bare bulb ceiling fixture. In his trips to Old Home Supply, Anthony had picked up a decorative globe to dignify that bare bulb.

"Hmmm," Clare mused, "all he needs are pictures. I'll have to talk to him about that."

The adjacent area, which Otto used as a kitchen/bedroom had cupboards loaded with coffee, dry cereal, a few easily heated canned goods—we wouldn't eat canned pasta but after all his eating out, Otto might enjoy it. Keisha had been judicious in her selection of staples. The under-the-counter refrigerator held fresh milk, orange juice, fruit, lettuce, and cheese. A new hot plate and chrome toaster oven sat next to each other on the counter, and for an extra touch Claire had picked up a bargain bundle of bright kitchen towels.

"We really ought to paint these rooms...."

"Claire, we've got enough to do."

Theresa, the girls and I had stocked the shelves with clocks in various stages of disrepair, carefully placing the labeled parts next to them. Anthony had gotten the glass company to put in new windows on Saturday without charging overtime. All in all, if you first walked in and didn't look closely, you'd think nothing had happened. Of course, a second glance would reveal the broken clocks but Otto would have to fix them. I could hear him in my mind now ranting about the barbarians who broke the clocks but enjoying exercising his own skill at fixing them.

We all gathered back at our house and sent Joe and José, who was off today and tomorrow, for carryout from the Grill and more beer. Claire ran home to get bottles to supplement the wine I had on hand. When she hurried back, clutching four bottles of wine, I reflected on how she had changed from the Claire I first knew who was always impeccably dressed in a matching outfit. This Claire's hair was escaping from her ponytail to form becoming tendrils around her face. Her makeup had mostly faded off, and her once-crisp striped shirt was wrinkled and dirty. She had frequently wiped her dirty hands on her jeans, and they too bore stains.

We drank a toast to what we had accomplished, and I almost felt guilty that Mom and Otto weren't with us. But I think that was Mom's choice, and maybe Otto didn't know he had a choice.

"Are we good or aren't we?" Mike asked, raising his beer in the air, to a chorus of cheers. I hadn't seen him this happy in a long time.

As we sorted out the food orders, I thought we should

have said turkey burgers for everyone all around—but then each one would have wanted his or hers a little differently. We settled to eat off paper plates, everyone content except Em who complained she got "regular" fries instead of curly. Maggie offered to share, but I gave her all mine—I didn't need fries, curly or straight.

The group decided collectively that all of us taking Otto to his shop would be overwhelming, and Mike and I were elected which meant, of course, that the girls would go with us. I called Mom about eight on Saturday night and asked what was for Sunday dinner.

"Why?" she asked suspiciously.

Taken a bit aback, I said, "We thought we'd invite ourselves for Sunday dinner. I know you want to go with us to show Otto his shop. And I just thought...." I was blathering.

Mom's reply? "Actually I thought I'd take him to brunch at Sapristi's."

"Oh, well, sure. We'll just meet you afterward. How about two o'clock at Otto's shop?"

She hesitated. "I'm sure that will be fine. Let me just check with Otto," and she turned away from the phone. I heard her in the distance saying something. Otto's reply came back more clearly, "I have to get back to my store, Cynthia." Mom came back on the phone and said almost crisply, "We'll be there at two."

Hanging up the phone, I looked at Mike and said, "I think Mom is reluctant to give up taking care of Otto."

He laughed. "Kelly, stop imagining romance everywhere." Then he shot me what was supposed to be a dark, romantic look, and said, "Keep the romance for us."

This time I laughed.

****

Otto was overwhelmed. He kept saying, "You did this for me?"

"Us and a small army," I said, naming all the others who had helped.

"I have not had real friends for years," he said. "Mr. Lattimore's greed may be the best thing that ever happened to me." He was thoughtful. "Of course, I may still have to kill him."

I wanted to clasp my hands over the girls' ears, but they just looked puzzled. I knew there would be questions later.

Mike, bless him, changed the subject. "How did we do, Otto? If any parts are mislabeled, I take full credit. I did all the sorting and labeling."

"I'm sure there will be some out of order, but nothing compared with what I saw Thursday night. I can fix it. And I never could have gotten all this cleaning done. You are miracle workers. I can go to work first thing tomorrow, maybe even tonight."

Mom had been inspecting the living quarters, which Otto hadn't even looked at. "I don't know how you can live here," she said almost petulantly.

Otto went into the two back rooms for the first time and said, "This is not my furniture."

"Yours was ruined," I said. "This is garage sale furniture, but Claire thought it was a bit of an improvement."

"I will live like a king," he said, sticking his head into the sleeping/kitchen area. He turned to Mom, "Cynthia, you have spoiled me, but we both know that couldn't go on. I have to come back to the store. I will miss your comfortable home and your good cooking, but this is where I belong. And now it's so much nicer than it ever has been."

Mom managed a smile, and said, "Of course, Otto. I'm pleased you're happy."

"You will come visit and I will make for you," he

looked in the cupboard, "spaghetti dinner."

We all laughed, and Mom said she'd enjoy it. They'd brought Otto's things from Mom's house, so after she asked him ten times if he was sure he'd be all right, we left him to get settled in. Mom actually did invite us back to her house for supper.

"I pulled a pork roast out to defrost this morning, and I have potatoes. Kelly, do you have salad makings?"

"No, but I'll get them." I thought it was a good thing she didn't mention including anyone else, especially Otto, for dinner. She needed some time with her granddaughters.

Later that night I reported to all those involved about Otto's reaction and told them I knew they'd be hearing from him directly. Weeks later he would present each of us with a carefully chosen clock. For Anthony, there was a clock with figures from Greek mythology on the face; for Keisha and José, a clock from Spain; for Claire, a lovely early nineteenth century chiming clock; and for Mike and me, a clock designed in the Craftsman period which fit our house perfectly. I never knew if Mom got a clock but I bet she got a special one.

****

All weekend, while we cleaned and worked, I'd hidden my anger, turning it into energy for the job at hand. I thought I'd fooled everyone, though I should have known that Mike wasn't blind to my motives.

As we lay in bed reading—me with the new Deborah Crombie mystery and he with David McCullough's new book about Americans in Paris, he put his book down and looked at me. "So what are you going to do, Kelly?"

"What do you mean?" I was honestly puzzled.

"I know you're not content to just clean up the mess at Otto's store and let the vandalism and beating go, even though they're police matters."

"Have the police got any leads?"

"I don't know." He shrugged. "I'm a desk employee, remember, and off for the weekend. But I know you won't let this go."

Caught! He knew me too well. I decided it was best to be honest with him. "I intend to march into Tom Lattimore's office tomorrow morning, unannounced, and ask him exactly what he thought he was doing and what he thought scaring Otto would accomplish."

"It doesn't seem to have accomplished a lot, except for ruining a lot of valuable old clocks. Otto isn't scared."

"No, but Tom Lattimore won't know that."

"I can't talk you out of this?"

"Of course not. The police can't confront Tom, because they don't have enough evidence. I don't have evidence, but I have my instinct, which you will remember is usually on target." I said the latter rather loftily.

"Kelly, one promise, please?"

I looked at him, and I knew my tone was a bit belligerent as I said, "What?"

"Take your gun in your jacket pocket and wear the damn jacket. The gun is not heavy enough to pull the pocket down and make it evident."

"Is my pants pocket okay?"

"If they're front-pleated pants with a roomy pocket. And be sure not to shoot yourself. Could be painful." He was playing with me now, and I slammed my book shut. And then his, causing him to howl that I'd lost his place.

Chapter Fifteen

Truth be told, I was scared about confronting Tom Lattimore. When I took the girls to class, I chattered so much that Em said, "Mom, why are you talking about all this stuff? You're usually so quiet in the morning. I need quiet to get ready for school."

"What's to get ready for second grade?" Maggie scoffed. "Now *fifth* grade is really hard."

"So is second," Em said, "and that wasn't nice of you Maggie."

I decided to shut up and drove the few blocks in silence.

At the school, I hugged each girl so fiercely they looked at me with questions in their eyes, but I just said, "Run along. Have a good day."

It was too early to go to Tom's office, so I went to my own. Keisha wasn't in yet, and I rattled around in the quiet, empty office, rehearsing what I'd say to Tom Lattimore. I wouldn't call ahead. I'd just count on catching him before he took off for the day.

Keisha came in, hung up her jacket and purse, looked at the pot of coffee I'd made and then at me with a quizzical look—I never made coffee. Finally she settled herself at her desk and asked, "Something I should know? Something happen between Saturday and this morning?"

I shook my head. "No, Otto was pleased as could be with his office and his new living quarters. I don't think Mom was so pleased to give him up, but we left Otto to settle in and all went back to Mom's for supper."

She waited, knowing I'd go on.

"I'm going to go talk to Tom Lattimore this morning."

Keisha sighed. "I knew you were bottling it up inside you all weekend. You're sure he was behind the attack on Otto?"

"Of course I'm sure. It never occurred to me to doubt it. He wants Otto out of there. I talked to the other shop owners, and they'd all had visits, but no one was as stubborn as Otto. Tanya wants to stay but she won't put herself and her child at risk. The sushi owner wasn't around and his manager didn't seem interested. The taqueria guy will move easily. I guess they don't have much emotion invested in their businesses or our neighborhood."

"You blame them, with what happened to Otto as an example? What if Lattimore says he didn't do it?"

I crumpled. I hadn't expected that, even thought of it. Of course he did it.

But that's just what he did. He denied it.

I walked to his office, since it was only three blocks or so. It was a lovely fall day, crisp and cool but with the sun promising heat later in the day. People greeted me on the street, and I had no thought for much except how lovely our neighborhood is. Such thoughts vanished when I approached Tom's office. Bella Garza was just leaving. She had the nerve—gall?—to look my way and wave. Then she climbed into the old green car and peeled off. In an instant, she took all my self-confidence with her.

My hand was shaking as I pushed open the door to Tom's office. His receptionist looked up, but Tom had glanced out the window of his private office, a space where he could keep watch on the street, and had seen me coming. He rushed into the reception area, both hands extended.

"Kelly, this is a pleasant surprise. Or did we have a meeting I forgot to write down?"

With a gesture, he showed me into his office then to a

cushy leather chair facing his desk. He sat opposite me and picked up a pencil to fiddle with and keep his hands busy.

I wondered if that was a sign of nervousness. "No, Tom, no appointment. I just walked down and took a chance on finding you in."

"I'm glad you did. I have to leave in, oh, thirty minutes or so, but what can I do for you now?"

"Why did you do it, Tom? Why send goons to beat up Otto Martin and trash his store and all those valuable antique clocks?"

"Kelly, back up. What are you talking about?"

"You know very well," I said, my voice rising.

Tom got up and closed his office door, then with a measured walk returned to his desk and picked up the pencil. "No, I honestly don't. Start from the beginning please. No, wait." He picked up his phone, punched a button, and said, "Carolyn, no calls. And cancel my nine-thirty appointment. I'll reschedule." Then he looked at me.

"Thanksgiving night," I said, "a holiday when we are all grateful. Otto got home and found his store vandalized. Clocks thrown everywhere, many of them I'm sure beyond repair, some of them probably pretty valuable. Thoughtless, mean vandalism. Then later that night, they came and beat Otto badly. He went to the ER at JPS—well, the police took him."

"The police?" He looked a little alarmed at that. "Is he all right now?"

"Yes, a bunch of us spent the weekend cleaning his store, and my mom fed him chicken soup and gave him TLC. He's not moving, Tom."

He put his hand to his forehead and stared at me. "Kelly, I had nothing to do with this, believe me."

I was stubborn. I *knew* he had something to do with it. "Why should I believe you? You threatened me. You as much as told me you'd do anything to get this deal to go through. Just how much is it worth to you, Tom?"

"Not that much," he said. "I didn't know about it, I didn't have anything to do with it. But I don't expect you to believe me."

I tried another approach. "I saw Bella Garza leaving here. What business do you have with her?"

"Who? Oh, that Mexican girl? She just came to deliver a message."

"Weak, Tom. Did you know she's been stalking me? Threatening me and my family? She says it's because of her sister's death, in the accident that involved my husband, but I think there's more to it. Bella hated her sister."

He began to pace. "Kelly, this is all too complicated for me. I don't know this Bella Garza, didn't even ask her name. She just brought me a message." He went to his desk and picked up a sealed envelope. "See? I haven't even read it yet. I saw you coming and put it aside."

"Why don't you read it, Tom?"

"No, I want to convince you first that I had nothing to do with beating that old man. Of course, he did say he'd kill me, but I didn't take that seriously."

Some instinct inside me pushed. "Read the message, Tom."

He looked startled, then sat down and slit open the envelope—with a sterling letter opener, of course. He read, and his eyes widened. Then he crumpled the letter, threw it on his desk, and said, "Kelly, I can't talk now, but you have to believe me. I didn't ask anyone to target Otto Martin. Now I've got to go. I'm sorry." He stood, clearly indicating that this little talk was over.

On the way back to the office, I kept looking over my shoulder, expecting to see Bella's car. I didn't, but I did see Tom jump in his Mercedes convertible and roar away from his office, before I was half a block away. Puzzled, I hurried back to the office. I couldn't wait to tell Mike about this, but I knew Keisha would pry the story out of me first.

She did, and I repeated it almost word for word, the way I remembered it. I expected wisdom from Keisha, but all she said was, "Don't that beat all? I suspect he didn't do it, Kelly. What now?"

I had no idea what now, but Bella solved that problem for me. She called the office within an hour. "Stay away from Tom Lattimore, Ms. O'Connell." Her voice dripped sarcasm when she called me by name. "There are people bigger than him who want this store on Magnolia, and they'll get it. I advise you to get out of the way *now*. Especially if you care about Maggie and Em."

That she knew my daughters' names chilled me to the bone. I hung up the phone, afraid to hear more.

Keisha was on her feet in a flash and by my side. "Kelly, what is it? You turned dead white." She always knew when to put the joking aside and take me seriously.

"Bella just threatened the girls," I stammered. "She says Tom Lattimore is a small player in this whole thing. Keisha, why would anyone want a grocery store on Magnolia that badly?"

"Beats me. To my thinking, grocery stores need to be near people, but location isn't that critical. They shouldn't need that particular spot."

"No, but if you think about it, there's not really any space on Magnolia for what Tom is proposing. I guess he's fixed on this place—or those bigger people have—as a sort of 'Do or die' thing." Little did I know I would come to regret those words.

"Kelly, you got to talk to Mike and Buck. Buck's been taking you serious these days. He'll listen."

"But what's to tell? The girls have been threatened. How does that change things? My sense is that Buck can't act until something happens—he can't anticipate a crime. And by the time he can, it's too late."

"So you got it all figured out and you're gonna to take care of it yourself?" Now she was scornful and not at all amused.

****

Before we could argue further, the office door opened and John Henry Jackson heaved his bulk inside and, after a nod at Keisha, sank into my visitor's chair, which creaked with his weight.

Looking straight at me, he said, "We got a problem, little lady."

I did not like being addressed as "little lady," but I kept my peace. "The Magnolia development," I responded.

"Why I like you. You're sharp. Yeah, the Magnolia Development. I'm getting some pressure from pretty heavy sources to approve it."

"But you won't," I replied, "because you're impartial, and your nine-member commission votes independently. How many votes can you count on?"

He let me assume he was on my side. "Don't know. We got at least a couple of ringers. From the far west side district, a Westover Hills society lady who don't give a whit about Fairmount. And there's the mayor's new appointee, developer named Jake Southerland."

Jake Southerland. My once-client who had switched to Tom Lattimore. The developer who thought preserving old buildings was sheer folly. What in heaven's name was he doing on the Landmark Commission? I refrained from asking that. "But with the other seven of you, you should have a clear majority."

"Should have and do have are different critters," John Henry said, wiping his brow with a huge handkerchief. "I'll keep working on it. Hear you got a little problem of your own. Someone stalking you?"

"Now where'd you hear that?"

"Word gets around that courthouse."

"I bet it does. Well, it's okay, John Henry. I can take

care of myself. When is the commission going to announce its decision on this development?"

"Christmas week. I'll keep doing what I can."

Christmas week wasn't all that far away. But there was nothing I could do, as far as I knew, to influence the commission. They made their decisions independently.

He heaved himself out of the chair and held out a pudgy hand. "Good to see you, little lady. You keep in touch and let me know if you need anything."

I rose. "Thanks, John Henry. You take care."

The minute he was gone, Keisha said, "Something about that man gives me the willies."

"For Pete's sake, Keisha, he's on our side. He just talks like a politician."

She shook her head, stood up and grabbed her purse. "Let's go."

"Where are we going? It's almost time to pick up Mike for lunch."

"We're goin' to your garage apartment. See how hard it will be for me to move in there, how much junk we're going to have to move. If even John Henry knows you're being stalked, we got to do something new."

"Hold on. If Mike can't protect us, what makes you think you can?"

"I got a weapon he doesn't, for all his guns."

I looked at her curiously.

"Sixth sense," she said calmly, turning off her computer and picking up her purse. "Come on. Then you and Mike can buy me lunch."

I followed obediently, leaving her to lock the office. We drove to the house in silence, until she asked, "Apartment locked?"

"Key's on my key ring."

"Okay. Drive down the driveway and we'll go directly out there."

Keisha was giving orders again. As I got out of the car, I noticed that Bella had pulled up behind us. Keisha turned around and waved almost friendly-like. "Want her to know I'm taking part in this," she said. Then she marched toward the apartment.

It wasn't as bad as she feared. The treadmill could be folded up and stashed against one wall, and I thought we could fit the bike into our bedroom—after all, the bedroom was a spacious room and maybe Mike would use it more if it were inside, once he was given permission.

"We'll have to talk to Mike," I said.

"We will."

I knew that meant she would.

We picked up Mike and headed for Lili's. I wanted the comfort of the house wedge with blue cheese and bacon dressing. If Mike was surprised to see Keisha, he said nothing. Nor did he ask what we were up to. When he heard, he would want to take care of us himself. I'd let Keisha explain sixth sense to him.

Lili's was a perfect choice. Mike couldn't explode. At the Grill, he might have felt freer to give vent to his anger. Instead he asked rhetorically, "How does that little bitch know stuff we can't find out? Buck's been investigating Lattimore, on the sly, and come up empty. Can't even link him to that North Side Properties you found out about, Kelly. That seems to be a front, a paper business."

"A paper business?"

"Covering up for some illegal activity. Besides gouging poor people for unreasonable rents."

"If it's that kind of operation, why did Tom call me back about Sonny Adams?"

"To throw you off," Keisha said.

How did she get so smart? "Throw me off what?"

"Your interest in Sonny Adams," Mike supplied. "My guess is that he was indeed skimming the top off rents and was killed as an object lesson to others. But we'll never find his killer if we can't find out who is behind North Side Properties."

I was beginning to feel naïve. "I thought it was Tom."

"A front," Keisha said.

Well, darn, why didn't she just join the police force?

We pushed our empty plates to the edge of the table, paid the bill, and were about to leave when I brought up Keisha and the apartment.

"Oh, yeah," she said casually to Mike. "I'm movin' in. Gonna help you protect your family."

Predictably he said, "I don't need help. I can take care of them myself. Even with a bad leg."

"You ain't got the sense," she replied.

He stiffened. "I don't have enough sense to take care of them?"

"No," she was laughing now, "you ain't got the sixth sense. I do. Besides right now I can run faster than you."

I didn't point out I could probably run faster than both of them, but I'd be running with a girl under each arm.

"When are you moving in?"

"Tonight, while José is on duty."

That brought a question about José to my mind. "Keisha, the girls...." I know, I know—Mike and I lived together in sin, but the girls knew we would marry and be a family. José and Keisha seemed, I thought, a different kind of thing.

"Kelly, he won't be spending the night. He's gonna take my apartment and move outta his mama's house. He just don't know it yet, but I'll tell him. And I don't have to move all my stuff. This isn't permanent, so relax, Mike."

He grinned at her. Mike had learned faster than I had that when Keisha made up her mind, you didn't argue with her.

"Not going to solve it sitting here," he said. "Kelly,

take me back to the office."

"No. Doctor's orders—and they haven't changed."

"Because I haven't seen him," he retorted. "He'd understand. Take me to the office. I won't stay all afternoon. Buck can run me home."

Back at the office, I was tense, watching the clock, determined to be at the school early and go in and get the girls before they got out on the school grounds. Maybe I'd have to explain to Susan Smith, the principal, and have the girls wait for me in the office. They'd be embarrassed to tears.

Keisha began to sing, "Christmas is coming, the geese are getting fat."

I stared at her. How could she think of Christmas with my girls in danger?

"Got to be thinking about it. What you giving the girls? Suppose Miss Claire will invite us all again?"

I didn't let on that I knew she was trying to distract me. I went along with it. "I think it's my turn to do a big dinner. We'll rearrange the furniture to make room."

"Good, we can plan it together. I think I'll buy the girls some cool clothes, maybe promise them a shopping trip as their present."

I began to make lists and when I looked at the clock, I was almost late for the girls. I flew out the door, calling "See you tonight" over my shoulder. When I got to the school, Bella was there in her car, parked across the street, just watching the kids in the schoolyard. My heart skipped a beat. I slammed the car into park, jumped out without bothering to lock up my car, and ran for the school.

I grabbed Em as she came out the door of her room, waved hastily to her teacher, and flew down the hall to Maggie's classroom. They were already outside. I dragged Em, who complained, "Mom, why are we in such a hurry?"

To my relief, Maggie was standing in a knot of girls,

with her teacher keeping a watchful eye. She waved at me, and I hugged Maggie so tightly she looked at me strangely. On the way to the car, Maggie kept trying to tell me something, but I just hurried her along and said, "Tell me later."

When I got both girls in the car, my purse was gone. *Swell, now she's got my credit cards, my social security number, checkbook—she can totally steal my identity.* The fifty dollars or so in cash didn't bother me. I slammed my hand on the steering wheel so hard it hurt.

"Mom, you're really acting weird," Maggie said. And Em echoed, "Yeah, Mom, you are."

"Sorry, girls. Something's bothering me."

"The lady in the green car? I saw her take your purse. I was trying to tell you that. I bet you can tell Mike and they can go after her."

There was no need. When we got home, my purse was lying on the doormat, with nothing missing, not even the cash.

Neither of the girls said a word as they watched me pick it up and check it, and I was silent too. All the time I was giving the girls snacks and getting them started on their homework, a part of my mind was puzzling about Bella. It was no use. She stole my purse as a way of saying, "Look what I can do." But why did she return it? Was it audacity? Surely there wasn't a kind streak in her. She didn't want to be friends. She had made it clear she was the enemy, a threat to my family. I decided to be grateful I had my purse intact and forget about it, except I'd be more wary from now on.

That was another problem: I thought I was being careful and cautious, and yet I'd let Bella push me into a panic where I acted without thinking. She was winning this battle of the wits. I had to stay calm and cool.

"Mom?" Em called. "I'm through with my homework.

Would you come check it so I can start on my Christmas list?"

"Good idea," I replied. "You start on that list. You too, Maggie."

"I'm not through with my homework. Fifth grade is a lot harder."

"Of course," I said soothingly.

My thoughts happily diverted to Christmas, I went off to call my extended family about Christmas dinner which was, after all, only two and a half weeks away. How had I let it creep up on me like this? I knew how—and why. Bella and the big-box development.

Mom and Claire both protested that they wanted to have dinner at their houses, but I prevailed, sure it was my turn. "I don't know, Kelly. Is your house big enough? You've collected so many friends." Mom, as usual, had just a bit of disapproval in her voice, as though I'd been collecting strays on the street. I reminded her that I'd include Otto, and she brightened.

"Well, I suppose you can rearrange the furniture and make room. I do think we should all sit at tables and not eat out of our laps on Christmas day."

"Absolutely, Mom. Keisha is staying in the garage apartment for a while, and she'll help me rearrange. I won't let Mike do it."

Her antenna went up. "She is? Why?"

My caution alert went up as high as her antenna. "Oh, she just thought it was a good idea for a while. José needs to get out of his mother's house, and he's moving into the apartment." I wondered what José had thought about that plan.

"Of course," Mom said. "Although I'm sure his mother will miss him."

Was that a subtle dig? No, she couldn't live with us. We'd drive her crazy, and she'd do the same to us.

184

The recipients of my other calls were much quicker to accept and soon it looked like I'd have the usual crowd for dinner—about sixteen of us. I began to make lists—a menu, seating arrangement, gifts, etc. Man, I had a lot of work to do in the next two weeks. I could get Mom to bake and freeze dinner rolls, and Anthony would bring dessert...my mind began assigning tasks.

Mike clumped into the room with his walker. "Having fun? You're grinning over whatever you're working on."

"Lists for Christmas. Planning dinner and gifts. We'll host here. That okay?" I guess I hadn't been married again long enough. It didn't occur to me to check with Mike before inviting everyone to our house, and it should have.

"Perfect," he said. "I love having them all here. You know that."

"You won't have to do much. I'll see to that. But you will carve the turkey, won't you?"

"I'd be offended if you let anyone else do it." He was thoughtful a minute. "Have you put Bella and Tom and all that mess out of your mind?"

"For the moment. I can't let them ruin the holidays for us."

"You think Bella will take a Christmas holiday?"

"No, but I want the girls—and us—to have as normal a life as possible."

Chapter Sixteen

Instead of taking a Christmas holiday, Bella stepped up her stalking campaign with threatening notes and those middle-of-the-night phone calls I'd come to dread. Still, with a few changes, we went about our lives as always, even sometimes taunting Bella by waving to her. Once I left a sack of cookies on the front porch with her name, and it disappeared. I didn't think a stray dog got it. In a way, I'd come to accept her presence as a part of my life, an unpleasant part but still just part of my day.

The notes, often slipped through our mail slot, were disturbing, sometimes predicting doom and gloom on a certain day, sometimes talking fire and destruction. To my surprise, these were all handwritten in a neat, concise hand, properly punctuated and with correct spelling. Bella was no dummy, and somewhere along the way she'd paid attention in school. I forbade the girls to open such notes, and as far as I know, they obeyed. I don't think they wanted to know any more about Bella.

The phone calls were less specific and therefore less scary. Mike took to answering the phone and always simply heard the click of a hang-up. If I did happen to answer, I mostly heard heavy breathing. The calls were, however, a major annoyance when they came in the middle of the night, sometimes at twenty-minute intervals—just long enough to get back to sleep before the next one. We disconnected the phone, and Mike kept his cell handy in case of an emergency call. I made sure Mom had that number, with strict orders to keep it confidential. Nonetheless, Bella found out that number and began to call. Mike and I were both suffering from sleep deprivation—another of Bella's tactics to wear us down. It worked, and we were too often cranky in the morning. Didn't Bella ever sleep?

I had shared, in confidence, our situation with Susan Smith, the principal, and now the girls waited for me every day in her office. They were allowed on the playground during recess only with strict supervision. None of this pleased them, and they fussed until Mike sat them down and had a talk with them.

Bella knew better than to claim she had been sent to pick the girls up for me, but there was the day the school nurse called to say that Em was in her office throwing up. I rushed up to the school and burst into the nurse's office.

"Where's Em?" I demanded.

Caroline Patrick, the nurse, looked at me blankly. "Em hasn't been in here today. Far as I know she's fine."

Frantic now. "But I got this call. She was in your office, throwing up."

Caroline laughed a bit. "Thank heaven, no. Haven't had one case of the throw-ups today." Seeing that I was coming unglued, she suggested gently, "Why don't you check her classroom?"

Of course. I did. And there she sat, head bent over whatever she was working on. I watched for a minute, but she didn't look up, never saw me, and I slunk away. I did manage to go back to Caroline Patrick and report that all seemed well and stumble through an apology.

She was puzzled. "I don't know who called you. They didn't use my name, did they?"

I nodded. Yes, they had used her name, but I knew darn good and well who had called. When I got into my car and checked my cell phone, there was a message from Bella: "Glad the little one was okay." A chuckle. "Hope she stays that way."

The implication was all too clear.

I could not, I repeated to myself, let her get to me. This was less a physical threat than a battle of the wills. I went by the Fiesta Market and bought a small pork roast, pre-seasoned, some new potatoes to do in the oven with rosemary and olive oil, and Romaine lettuce for a Caesar salad. We would eat well tonight and pretend Bella didn't exist.

"What's the occasion?" Mike asked as he cut the small roast into slices.

"Nothing. I just felt like fixing a good dinner."

He and the girls wolfed it down and raved about it, and I was glad I had done it.

"Next time you get this urge, we really should call Nana," Mike said. "We don't see enough of her. And the girls don't see her enough."

"Sure," I said. "You're right. Let's talk later and plan something."

"Later" came after the girls were in bed and, I hoped, asleep. "Mike, Mom wants the girls to spend Friday night at her house."

"Great. A night alone for us." He tried his best to leer at me but his interpretation of a leer left a lot to be desired.

"But with this Bella business, I'm just not comfortable with that."

Mike didn't answer right away, and I was relieved that he didn't just brush away my hesitation. "Okay. What can we do to make it work?"

Finally I said in a questioning voice, "Keisha?"

"I'm okay with that, if you are. And if Nana and Keisha are. We'll have to coordinate schedules."

Keisha was actually delighted. Mom resented having to have a babysitter watch her when she thought she was babysitting, but she acquiesced, and it was arranged that the girls would spend the next Friday night at Nana's. My mom pumped them up with plans for things to do—make homemade ice cream, bake cookies. What child could resist? I tried hard to quiet my worries, and Mike tried equally hard to reassure me.

"Bella is not going to burst in there with a gun and start shooting," he said. "And Keisha can more than handle everything else. I'm fine with it."

"Okay. I am too." I said it with a bravado I didn't really feel.

That Friday night Keisha drove the girls to Mom's, after much hugging and kissing and assurances we'd meet each other in the morning for breakfast at Ol' South.

After they left, Mike grumbled, "For Pete's sake, it's not like they're leaving for a month. They'll be home in the morning."

"I know. But they haven't spent many nights away from me, and with Bella in the picture, I'm still nervous."

"Quit worrying. Let's go see if we can get a table at Nonna Tata."

We did. Took a bottle of red wine with us, held hands across the table while we waited for our pasta, and had a real, grown-up "date" kind of an evening. I only called Mom twice during dinner and once after we got home, when she assured me the girls were sound asleep. She and Keisha were watching TV and José had been by three times on his rounds. They were safe. No sign of Bella.

Keisha's parting words were, "You two stay safe."

"You too," I said, thinking it was just a nice way of saying goodnight. As it turned out we weren't safe. We just didn't know it.

About three, the sound of breaking glass woke both of us, bringing Mike to his feet too rapidly. He fell, and I struggled to help him to his feet.

"Get me the walker," he said. It had scooted away when he fell. As I pulled it back, he used the bed to pull himself up and said desperately, "I smell something. Living room."

I flew ahead of him down the hall until he said, "Stop, Kelly. Let me go first." He had his service revolver in one hand and used the other to clump the walker along. I ran back to the bedroom for my cell phone.

"Smoke bomb," he yelled. "Go out the back door. "

"You can't make it down those steps, and the front door is closer."

"Kelly, go out the *back* door now!" His tone told me not to argue with him, and I fled to the back door, hearing the walker behind me. Once outside I turned to help him, but he brushed me away and between the walker and the railing, he made it into the yard.

Only then did I call 911 and yell "smoke bomb." The operator, doing as she'd been trained, tried hard to keep me on the phone, but I didn't listen. I gave her the address and set the phone down. My focus was on Mike.

Winded by his exertion, Mike finally said, "Sometimes a smoke bomb is meant to scare you out in the open where you're a perfect target. Like tear gas."

Bella wouldn't shoot us —or would she? She didn't carry a gun. I heard sirens approaching then José's voice calling our names.

"In the back yard, José," Mike called.

He came bursting through the gate. "White smoke is pouring out of your house. Doesn't look like a fire."

"No fire," Mike said. "Smoke bomb. You didn't pass a battered green Mustang did you?"

"Man, I don't know what I passed. Once the call came through I just drove like hell."

"José, can you go through and open the front door, so the fire guys don't break it? Grab a wet paper towel in the kitchen for your nose."

José took off and apparently just made it to the front

door in time. In seconds, the house swarmed with firemen opening doors and windows. One of them had disarmed the bomb, and it was taken for evidence. The fire captain came out and reported to Mike that it was homemade, but in a canister that fragmented when it exploded. If anyone had been in the living room, they'd have been hit by flying fragments of metal. I made a mental note to examine the furniture and call poor David Summers, my usually patient insurance agent. José reported that the fire guys had set up giant fans inside.

We waited outside, shivering, but José finally brought us coats that smelled not like smoke but strangely chemical.

"I've got to call Keisha," he said.

"Don't wake them all up. They don't know anything's wrong."

"Keisha will know," he said archly, and he was right. She did. He handed me the phone.

"I knew I shouldn't have left tonight. Knew something would happen."

"Keisha, you couldn't have done anything."

"Don't be so sure. I'm gonna catch that girl red-handed one of these days. You just watch."

"Are the girls still asleep?" I prayed for a yes but got the opposite.

"Can't you hear them? They're standing right here, demanding to know what happened. Heard the phone ring. They want to come home."

Sigh. "Tell them home is too smoky—not fire smoke but something that smells awful. I think we'll sleep in the apartment, if you don't mind."

"'Course I don't mind. Doubt you'll sleep much anyway, but you try. We got work to do tomorrow, and I may have to do some detectin'."

She put the girls on, and I assured each one that Mike and I were freezing and frightened but okay.

"Can't we come home?"

"No, Em, you're better off with Nana and Keisha."

"Nana's crying and talking about moving back to Chicago."

That's all I need! Mom would harp on this for weeks. Finally I got the girls to go back to bed. "Keisha, tell Mom I'll talk to her tomorrow. I don't have the strength for it now."

She chuckled. "Miss Cynthia gonna be fine. I'll take care of that. You sleep now. You're safe."

I had to believe Keisha once again seemed to have that pipeline or sixth sense or whatever.

Mike finally thought to ask José what he was doing on patrol so late. His shift should have ended hours ago.

"You know that girl that's been stalking you? I arrested her tonight for loitering—outside Nonna Tata. I'm guessing that's where you had dinner."

I stared at him. "If she's in jail, she didn't throw the smoke bomb."

"Naw, she made bail about one. I was sort of footloose—Keisha being at your mom's and all, and I just hung around playing poker with a couple of the other off-duty guys." He looked anxious. "Don't tell Keisha. She doesn't like me to bet." That was the farthest thing from my mind right then, but I promised.

Mike was mumbling to himself, "She could still have done it, but she had to have help. You search her car when you hauled her in?"

"Sure. No smoke bomb."

"So somebody brought it to her. She's got help. She didn't have time to make a bomb, even if she knows how."

"Her brother?"

Mike shook his head. "I don't think he's a big enough player. He sure isn't smart enough to make a smoke bomb. My gut tells me someone else is pulling these strings. Bella may not have done this at all."

That was a disquieting thought. I wanted to tell him to ask Keisha but instead I asked, "How do you make a smoke bomb?"

Mike looked at me briefly. "Combination of chemicals—and simple things like sugar and sodium bicarbonate. Usually use potassium nitrate—probably what you smell."

It was five before everyone left. The fire department had boarded up the broken window and left someone to keep watch because they left the doors and windows open. As we fell into bed, I said, "Mike, Conroy didn't show up tonight. That's a first."

"Maybe no one called him," he said and was instantly asleep. I almost hated him as I fought to clear my mind and let sleep come.

We slept until almost ten and might have slept longer if someone hadn't pounded on the apartment door. Mike and I looked at each other. At least we knew it wasn't Bella—this person was not at all stealthy. Still as I said, "I'll go," Mike's hand reached for his revolver. Having no robe with me and sure that Keisha's caftans would swallow me, I put on the coat I'd worn last night and called, "Just a minute."

It was Buck Conroy, as we both should have known. "Getting your beauty sleep?" he asked as he barged in.

Mike sat up in bed. "We were up a good bit of the night."

"So was I. Tracking down where Bella Garza is and where she went after she posted bail."

"And?"

"She didn't do this. I had them put a tail on her, and he followed her to that old warehouse where we've found her before. She and Ben were both there. Officer held them until I got there. She was surly as usual but claimed she didn't know anything about this. You know what? I can spot a liar, and this time she wasn't lying. So now we got to figure out who did throw that bomb."

I shivered and drew the coat closer.

"For starters," Mike said, "could you let us get dressed and maybe meet us at Ol' South, say in half an hour? We're supposed to meet the girls, Keisha and Nana."

Conroy looked startled but said, "Oh, yeah, sure. A family party. Just what I need right now. I'll just go drink some more coffee."

I used my cell to call Nana and ask them to meet us at Ol' South. The girls of course had to talk, but I assured them we'd see them in thirty minutes and our talk was brief.

Everything in the house smelled funny, but not nearly as bad as last night. Mike commented, "Good thing about a smoke bomb—the smell goes away pretty quickly."

Unshowered and exhausted, we arrived at Ol' South. I ordered corned beef hash and two poached eggs, while Mike went for the full steak and eggs treatment. Conroy kept drinking his black coffee, and I wondered that his hands didn't shake from caffeine nerves. The girls greeted us with joyful hugs and protests about how much they missed us. Nana stood looking sort of wistful, while Keisha was busily efficient.

"You girls sit right here and tell me what you want." They wanted pigs in a blanket of course. Keisha ordered Dutch babies, and Nana said primly she'd already eaten breakfast. *Oh oh, the old Nana was back.*

"Okay, let's pool our knowledge. Kelly, I suspect you know things I don't." Conroy ignored the rest of my gathered family. He hadn't even greeted the girls, which gave me real doubts about his fathering abilities.

I bristled but told him about Tom Lattimore and the way he'd rushed from his office, looking scared or worried. And about Bella hinting at someone much "bigger" than

Lattimore, to which Mike said, "Not hard to be bigger than that little twerp."

I gave him what I hoped was a withering look. "What I can't figure out is why someone's so desperate about a grocery store at that location. Why not just move it rather than fight the preservationists and the landmark commission and all that red tape?"

"Maybe that's where the answer lies," Conroy mused. "Lattimore's the key. We've got to crack him." But he took the idea no further, and I was left stymied.

Chapter Seventeen

Tom Lattimore called me Monday after the bomb incident. He was, I thought, trying to sound upbeat and not quite pulling it off. "Kelly, I hate what happened at your house the other night. How bad is the damage?"

The Fairmount grapevine—no six degrees of separation in our neighborhood! "Some scratches to furniture from flying metal fragments and one torn chair. It can all be fixed."

"Well, thank God no one was hurt, and the girls weren't home."

How did he know that? Boldly, I asked him, "How did you know about it? Was it in the paper?"

"No. Nothing in the paper. Maybe Keisha told me. I called her yesterday to check on you. You weren't in the office. Anyway, the reason I'm calling is that we've got to put an end to this. I can't feel responsible for putting you in danger."

"Are you?" I was not playing games with him anymore.

"Inadvertently, maybe. Can we meet? I don't want to come to the office—I think the walls have ears."

"Keisha can be trusted," I said. "I tell her everything."

He laughed nervously, "Well, I hope not everything. No, that's not what I meant. I just think it's better if we meet some place unlikely."

Something dinged in my head. There was someone he didn't want to know he was meeting me. Couldn't be Bella, because she followed me everywhere. In fact, I was beginning to think I'd miss her when this all ended. And wouldn't Bella report back to whoever Tom was hiding from? Maybe if I met him he'd open up about North Side Properties. I had friends with a café in the Stockyard District on the North Side—maybe that was enough off the beaten path that he'd agree. I suggested the Star Café.

"No, not the North Side," he said too hastily.

I began to picture him on the other end of the phone, nervously twisting a pencil in his hands, sweating a little and wiping his forehead with his handkerchief. I was making this as difficult as I could.

"Okay," I said slowly. "How about The Lunch Box in Ridglea?"

"Perfect. Today? Eleven-thirty?"

"I'll be there," I said, and then, "I may bring Keisha."

"Uh, well, if you're sure...."

"I'm sure. Get a table for three."

We'd stand out like a sore thumb in The Lunch Box, a place with wonderful tuna and chicken and egg salad sandwiches plus other delights. The gray-haired crowd pretty much dominated there, and there were almost no men younger than sixty-five. Plus it wasn't usually very racially diverse. *What fun,* I thought as I turned to tell Keisha of our lunch plans.

"Did Tom Lattimore call yesterday and talk to you about the smoke bomb?"

She shook her head.

"Well, he says you're the one who told him the girls weren't home. Just keep that little secret under your bonnet. We're having lunch with him today."

"I don't want lunch with that scum," she protested.

"Be sweet."

"Someplace good?" She was hoping perhaps for Patrizio's or one of the other upscale places that had opened in the So7 district.

"Yep. The Lunch Box."

"Sandwiches," she sighed. "I eat enough tuna salad to

deplete the tuna in the ocean."

"So order chicken."

I called Mike and asked him to have Conroy drive him home, reminding him we had a four o'clock appointment with his surgeon. It was time anyway, but I wanted to be sure he hadn't done any damage the night the bomb went off. He was still only at about six months post-op, not ready to be dancing yet.

"Where are you going?" he asked suspiciously.

"To lunch with Tom Lattimore." Before he could object I added, "I'm taking Keisha. After all, Conroy wants to follow up."

The Lunch Box was sort of buried down an outdoor corridor in a huge shopping center in the Ridglea area along Camp Bowie. If you didn't know it was there, you'd never find it, but lots of people find it daily. I doubted the menu had changed in thirty years and maybe not the personnel. It was a sunny, cheerful, tea-room type of place, surely not the place to be discussing smoke bombs and stalkers and other threats. Yet there we were—Tom had, probably deliberately, gotten there early enough to get us a table in a corner. I decided he had a thing about corner tables.

He rose to greet us, kissed me on the cheek (yuck!) and took Keisha's hand in both of his. I thought she'd wince, but she played it like a trooper. Tom did look a little more disheveled, a little less arrogant than usual. His tie was loosened and crooked. He'd thrown off his jacket, and even in this cold he had sweat stains in the armpits of his shirt.

Stress! He's really stressed. My job is to find out why.

While we waited for our sandwiches, I said, "Okay, Tom, let's put our cards on the table. What can we do to stop this, other than removing all opposition to the big-box store?"

A nervous laugh. "Well, of course, that would make everything better, but I think it's gone too far for that."

"How about finding an alternative site?"

"I'm afraid they don't want that—they're set on that site."

"Okay, let's get real here. Who are 'they'?"

He squirmed in his chair, looked around nervously, and said, "Kelly, I don't know. I get instructions."

Keisha looked at him scornfully. "You just a gofer? I thought that's what my kind did."

He ignored her until I changed the subject.

"Tell me about North Side Properties."

He looked startled. "It's my company that handles rentals on the North Side. One reason I didn't want to go up there today."

Keisha again. "Why? You got so many disgruntled renters they might attack you in a simple café?"

"It's not that...."

"Wait a minute, Tom. You don't own North Side Properties, do you?"

He drew himself up. "A portion of it, yes, I do."

"What portion?"

He was fiddling with his iced teaspoon and now he almost threw it on the table. "For Pete's sake, Kelly, that doesn't matter now. I just don't own a controlling interest."

"Do you think whoever does had Sonny Adams killed?" I was really getting good at grilling.

The waitress arrived with our sandwiches, and we all three shut up and began to eat. Then I repeated my question.

"Yeah, I do think that's possible, Kelly, Keisha, but I don't want that to go any further. Adams was skimming off the top of the rents he collected."

"Yeah, you told me that. But you just said he was let go, not that he was killed because of it."

"Kelly, what you need to know is that there are people behind this who won't listen to me, won't let anything get in their way. They want that property."

Keisha asked the question I'd been about to, but as she asked, her open dislike of Tom was evident. "Why that property? There's lots of places to put a grocery store."

"They don't want any other property. They want that corner."

"Why?"

"I don't know."

I wasn't sure if he was lying or not. But we weren't getting anywhere, and I was through with my sandwich. "We seem to be stalled. The only way to stop this harassment—and danger to my family—is to allow the development, which really isn't in my hands anyway. Things have gone too far with the zoning commission and landmark commission and even the neighborhood to do that. What exactly is it that you think I can do to pull your chestnuts out of the fire? I sense I'm not the only one in trouble here."

He nodded. "You're not. I admit it. I guess what I want to know is if there is any way to use the concept of adaptive re-use to pull this project through?"

"Adaptive re-use to build a big-box store?" I exploded so loudly that he looked around, and I did see a few heads turn. Well, be darned!

"We talked once about putting the store in the existing historic buildings. All it would take is remodeling, and I kind of like the idea—sort of kitschy. Different departments in different buildings—produce in one, meat in another, you know."

"And you think kitschy is a good thing?" Keisha chimed in. "It means a cheap imitation."

"I didn't know that." He did look surprised. Then, defensively, "Well, I still think it's a good idea."

The waitress came with our check, and for once Tom didn't grab it in the grand gesture. I waited and finally took it.

"I'll leave a tip," he said.

I refrained from a sarcastic, "Gee, thanks," but I did say, "We aren't through here." There was a wait for tables—I could see the crowd by the door—but I wasn't leaving. "You want me to persuade all those tenants—including Otto Martin who intends to kill you—to give up their leases so the other owners and I can sell?"

"Otto Martin is the least of my worries," he said hastily. "I mean, yes, that's what I want. Most of them have agreed, and I don't want any more goons visiting any of the others."

"Why?" Keisha asked. "Because it might be traced back to you?"

"No, because I don't want people hurt. I'm done here." He threw some money on the table and left abruptly by a side door. We rose more leisurely, and I paid at the cashier's stand.

On the way home, I said, "Christmas is less than a week away." It would fall on Sunday this year, and I thought Keisha and I deserved to close down the office for a few days. I had most of my shopping and about half the wrapping done—hard to find the privacy to wrap without someone peeking. And I needed to start on some baking. Toward the end of the week, I'd make a massive grocery trip—I'd already ordered the fresh turkey—and start cooking. "Let's take this afternoon and tomorrow to wrap up things, and then we'll close until a week from tomorrow."

"A whole week? Boss lady, you're gettin' soft. But I like it!"

So that afternoon, we ploughed through paperwork, and I made phone calls to people with pending deals telling them we were closing for a week. I also called John Henry to ask about the Landmark Commission.

"I think I've got the votes," he said. "Never can be sure, but I think it's wrapped up. We announce tomorrow."

I felt pretty smug about all we'd accomplished and thought probably we'd get away by noon the next day. I could get a lot done before the girls got out of school Thursday afternoon for the holidays.

Everything changed Tuesday—or Monday night. Mike's phone rang in the night. He muttered a few things and said, "Yeah, see you in the morning." Then he shook me gently and said, "Conroy. Tom Lattimore's office was bombed last night."

"Another smoke bomb?"

"No, Kelly. A firebomb. Like a homemade Molotov cocktail. Office and all his records completely destroyed. Fireman saved the other two offices in the building—a dentist and a lawyer. Conroy's keeping me in the loop even though officially it's none of my business." After a minute, he added. "Nor your business."

Even Mike, who could always sleep, lay awake. After a while he went to put on a pot of coffee, even though it was four-thirty in the morning.

I lay figuring, or trying to. Was this to scare Tom or was there something in his records someone wanted destroyed? I guess we'd never know unless Tom himself told us, and that wasn't likely.

I refused to get up at four-thirty. It was against my principles. I heard Maggie go into the kitchen and then soft murmurings as Mike led her back to bed. I lay there. Mike came back to bed but didn't sleep. When the alarm went off at six-thirty, we were both awake but exhausted and a bit cranky.

I threw on jeans and a big shirt and started bacon and eggs for the girls, while Mike oversaw their teeth brushing and dressing. Em dressed with her own definite style but Mike wasn't sure it was appropriate for an ordinary school day and urged her to save the tiered skirt and sparkly top for the last day of school and put on her jeans. She refused, and I arbitrated with a cross, "Oh, for heaven's sake. Let her wear what she wants." There was talk of citywide uniforms for public school next year, and I'd be glad if they were adopted.

The girls picked at their food. Maggie wanted to know details of what had happened last night, and Em pouted because no one woke her up. I told them both we didn't know any more than we'd told them, and we'd let them know when we did. Such an education my girls were getting!

"Mom, will somebody bomb your office next?" Em asked seriously.

"No, darling. Why would they?" But the thought had occurred to me. Except Tom and I were on different sides of this issue, so, logically, if someone bombed his office, they'd want to support me. *Logic doesn't work in this case.*

Tom called the house just as I was getting the girls into the car. "Can't talk, Tom. Late for school, but I'm devastated about what happened to your office. I'll call your cell in about fifteen minutes."

"As soon as you can," he said, "I need help."

Help? What kind of help could he need from me?

I dropped the girls off first and then took Mike to the substation. "Call me right away and let me know what Lattimore wants," he said.

The shoe, I thought, was on the other foot. I was the one with information—or would be—and he wanted it from me. If it weren't so serious, I'd have laughed. Between the substation and the office, I picked up Bella. I drove by Tom's office and sure enough, it was gutted and still smoldering. That the fire department had been able to protect the other part of the building was amazing. When I got to my office, I made a u-turn in a nearby parking lot and then parked in front of the office. Bella parked across the street, and when I waved, she almost waved back.

Keisha made no pretense about minding her own business, quizzing me the minute I walked in the door.

"How did you know?"

"José," she said. "He called first thing this morning, before I met him for breakfast."

"I have to call Tom first. He said it was urgent."

She scooted right into my visitor's chair, eyes as alert as her ears.

Tom answered immediately. "Kelly, thanks for calling right back. I need help. I'm scared."

"Is your office a total loss?"

"That's almost inconsequential. I don't even care about my business. I'm worried about my life."

I drew in a sharp breath. "Your life? Is it unraveling?"

"Yeah, but more than that. I think it may end. Kelly, I'm scared. After last night I think something might happen to me."

"Like what?"

"Do I have to spell it out?" He was irritated, edgy, about to come unglued. "I think someone's trying to kill me—or will be."

Lord help us...or him. "Tom, are you over-reacting to last night? If someone wanted to kill you, they'd have bombed the office with you in it."

"Not in the daytime. I'm scared, Kelly. I'm asking you for help."

"Where are you?"

"I can't tell you that. But I'm safe...for now."

"Will you talk to Buck Conroy?"

"He scares me."

"Tom, you're going to have to talk to someone about it, someone who can do something. I can't. Please. I can have Mike arrange a meeting someplace you think is safe.

Just not under a bridge at midnight with just the two of you."

"Not funny. I'm not in the mood for jokes."

"Sorry. It was only half a joke. It's got to be someplace safe for Mike—or else you've got to include Conroy."

"I can't come to your house even late. Bella would see me."

So Bella's now the enemy. Interesting.

"You name the time and place."

"I...I can't think right now. I'll call you tomorrow."

Before I could say I'd be home and not at the office, he hung up.

"Wish you had speaker phone," Keisha said. "Tell me what he said. I gather he's scared...and well he should be."

"I've got to call Mike. You listen. Take notes if you want."

She went to her desk for a legal pad and returned, pen poised in the air.

I repeated my conversation with Tom word for word, or as close as I could come. Keisha scribbled furiously. When I finally wound down, he said, "Kelly, I think his life probably *is* in danger. Trouble is we don't know from whom. Not Bella."

"She's parked outside," I said, "or was when I came in."

"Yeah, and he mentioned Bella would know if he came to the house. I read into his words that Bella would tell someone, and I suspect the last thing he needs now is for that someone to know he's talking to police." He was silent for a while. "Wait a few hours and call his cell again. See if you can find out where he is. I'm worried about him, not that I like the guy. But he's our clue to what's going on. Wish we could identify the powers behind North Side Properties—I think the key is there."

"Me too," I said. So much for working a half day.

John Henry called, his voice low and confidential. "Kelly, I couldn't swing it. The commission voted to approve the new plan—adaptive re-use instead of demolition—and send it back to the zoning board. I guess you'll have to live with it."

Sigh. "I'm disappointed, John Henry, but thanks for doing what you could. Guess we'll have to put up a fight again with the zoning board."

"Don't know that you'll win this time, Kelly. Sometimes you got to take your licks."

Not for a big-box store on Magnolia, no matter how innovative it is.

"One more thing, Kelly. Lattimore will be notified through official channels, but that's slow. Why don't you give him a call?"

"You know his office was bombed last night, don't you?"

"Read it in the paper. I'm sorry as preservationists we have a fringe element that would go that far. I know you know him, so be a good girl and call him with good news."

I didn't particularly feel like being a "good girl" for John Henry but I was worried about Tom, and I agreed.

Keisha, of course, was bursting with curiosity, and when I told her the commission decision, she turned indignant and angry, exploding with "How can they? Somebody's got them in his pocket."

"I don't think Tom's pockets are that deep," I said, dialing his cell phone. He didn't answer, and I left as upbeat a message as I could manage, telling him I had good news. Then I called Mike.

He was disappointed, but he said philosophically, "Win some, lose some, Kelly. Just like you can't save the whole world, you can't win all your preservation battles."

I did not want the philosophical acceptance of Mike or John Henry. I wanted Keisha's indignation. *How could they, indeed!*

We talked about what O'Connell and Spencer Realty could do to help Tom—if that wasn't extending the olive branch, I'll never eat another olive! Finally, reluctantly, we both decided to offer Tim's old desk, long vacant, to Tom to start rebuilding his work. He'd have a base, a desk, a phone, and not much privacy.

I tried to call him again, but still no answer. This time my message was actually a little more upbeat. I told him I had a plan.

When it was time to get the girls, I hadn't heard from Tom and I was worn out emotionally. Bella followed me to the school then, when I had the girls in tow, to our house, but I was too exhausted to worry about her.

I fixed a lackluster hamburger casserole for supper by dumping in mushroom soup, browned hamburger, cooked noodles, a can of tomatoes, and whatever spices struck my fancy. Then I topped it with cheese, which all ran down into it because the mixture was so soupy. It wasn't my best effort, and Maggie asked, "Is it stew or casserole?" Mike suggested maybe he was strong enough to take over cooking again, but he was joking and gentle. He knew I was upset.

In truth, I didn't know which bothered me more—the commission or Tom's silence. Finally about eight, I said it aloud. "Mike, I'm worried about Tom."

Calm as always, he said, "I am too, Kelly. If he's as upset as you thought and looking to you for help, he should have called. Maybe he's holed up somewhere drinking himself to oblivion."

"He drinks, sure, but I never saw him drunk. I don't think he likes to lose control."

"We can't count him as a missing person—no one's reported him, and he did say he was hiding. I'll talk to Conroy in the morning."

Morning might be too late! Kelly, stop dramatizing!

Chapter Eighteen

Next morning I had great plans for using all that free time with the office closed, the girls at school, and Mike at the substation. Instead, I decided to go back to bed.

"Kelly, I don't like leaving you alone in the house," Mike said as we neared the substation. "Things are too uncertain right now. Especially with Lattimore missing."

"Don't be silly, Mike. I'll be fine. I just need quiet time alone—and a bit more sleep. Then I'll start on Christmas."

"I'm not being silly," he said stubbornly. "Promise me you'll take precautions."

"Okay. I'll lock the doors, turn on the alarm, keep my phone by the bed."

"And your handgun."

Bother! I'm not going to shoot anyone. "And my handgun."

"Check and be sure it's loaded."

He almost managed to scare me. I began to wonder if he had Keisha's sixth sense, but I decided he was just worried. If I'd been in danger, Keisha would have called.

Going back to bed in the morning—a rare occurrence—never produced sleep for me, more dozing. Half of my mind actively made plans, figured things out, organized my life. This morning, I was thinking about Christmas and all I had to do. The other half of my mind was thinking how cozy and comfortable I was, even without Mike in the bed. Gus was curled at my feet, something Mike never allowed, and was sleeping soundly.

At first, I heard just a light scratching, so faint I wasn't sure what it was. Gus slept on, so nothing alarmed him. But then I heard a few more, slightly louder noises that I couldn't identify. I could tell the noises came from the front door. Without even realizing I did it, I picked up the gun and crept to the bedroom door. I had a perfect view of the hall and the door into it from the living room. Anyone who approached my bedroom would have to come through that door.

Within seconds, I heard that squeak—I never had used WD40 on the front door, in spite of good intentions, and now I was grateful. A whispered oath—whoever it was must have barked a shin on the heavy Craftsman furniture. A whispered, "Shhh," followed. Two people!

I was sure my heartbeat had slowed to zero and I was about to go into cardiac arrest from fear. My hands trembled—could I shoot the gun if I had to? My knees felt weak and I leaned against the doorframe, listening with maybe the greatest concentration I'd ever given anything. I heard them going through the house, quietly but with an occasional mis-step. If I'd been sound asleep, I never would have heard it. Gus still didn't budge, except to twitch his ears as he dreamt.

The house was dark, and they surely would figure that I was sleeping. They'd head for the bedroom, and I'd have one chance—only one. I straightened up and in so doing strengthened my resolve and my steadiness. I was in total dark whereas whoever came through that door would be backlit by the winter daylight streaming into the living room. I assumed that ridiculous pose Mike had taught me and waited. *What in the hell are they doing that's taking so long?*

In truth, they probably hadn't been in the house three minutes when a tall, bulky figure stood in the doorway from the living room, probably fifteen feet from me. No hesitation. I fired, and he clutched his belly and crumpled.

Behind him, Bella screamed, "Bitch! You shot him. You shot my brother!"

"Stop right there, Bella, or I'll shoot you too." It was, I

told myself, like target practice though there was a lot more at stake.

Bella moved a step toward me, and for a surreal moment it reminded me of the moving targets Mike had used. I shot, and she screamed in pain and staggered into the doorframe.

"My shoulder! Damn! You bitch!"

I held the gun on her, wondering how I was going to control her and retrieve my phone from the bedroom. Bella solved that problem for me—lurching and clutching her right shoulder with her left hand, she fled out the door. In her haste, she dropped a wicked looking knife.

Her brother hadn't moved, but he moaned, so I knew he was alive. *Thank the Lord!*

I kept my wits about me long enough to call 911, give the operator the address, tell her two people were shot, one fled. She kept talking, but I put the phone down, grabbed Gus who had wakened finally, and sobbed into his coat while he licked my face.

That's how Conroy found us. He ran down the hall shouting my name.

"In here," I said. Behind him I heard the clump of the walker, a muttered "Damn!" and then, "Conroy, I need help. Come get me. She's my wife, dammit!"

I looked down the hall and saw that Mike's way was blocked by Ben's inert form. Conroy must have jumped over him. I ran to Mike, who threw the walker away and held me in his arms. Once in that wonderful comforting place I began to cry all over again. Mike stroked my hair, murmured reassurances, and let me sob.

Conroy was not so patient. "Okay, everyone. In the living room. We got business."

The paramedics arrived and went straight to Ben. I couldn't bear to look while they worked over him, and I put my hands to my ears to block what they were saying to each other. Gently, Mike took my hands down.

"It's okay, Kelly. He'll most likely live. You were a little wide on your shot"—he tried to grin—"and didn't hit any vital organs."

I slumped against him. "Bella?"

Conroy had stepped outside and now came back in. "They found her in her car about a block away, about to pass out from loss of blood. She'll be okay, but her shoulder never will be any good. High and wide, Kelly."

"The gun kicked on the second shot," I said defensively. It was probably the first sensible thing I said, and I have no idea where it came from, but I remembered feeling the gun kick up as I fired that second shot. Thank goodness, or I might have killed her.

Mike pulled me to the couch and sat with me, while Conroy wandered into the kitchen. "You got anything stronger than wine?" he called.

"Bourbon," Mike answered. "Top shelf, cupboard over the sink."

Conroy brought me two fingers neat, with an order to sip. I did, but the warmth did little to cure the cold feeling that had come over me. I had shot two people. What would I tell the girls? How could I ever live with this? If either of them died—I put that thought aside. Mike said they wouldn't.

Conroy waited patiently for maybe two minutes and then said, "Tell me what happened, minute by minute."

I tried, my voice halting, and he interrupted with questions. My mind swam with little things I couldn't remember. What was the first sound I heard? How long between the time they entered the house and the time Ben stepped into the hall?

"An eternity," I said. And then for no reason added, "Mike, I think Gus is deaf. He didn't bark, didn't budge."

He relaxed just a bit for the first time. "We'll get his

hearing checked, but not right now."

"Forget the dog," Conroy said harshly. "Do you realize these two punks meant to kill you?"

I stared at him. "The thought went through my mind. That's why I shot." I looked at Mike. "You were right about Bella all along. She's beyond hope."

He put his finger to my lips. "She won't threaten you again. She'll be gone for a long time."

"There'll be an investigation, and the house is a crime scene. Got to block it off." Buck began to issue orders. "Mike, call Keisha. Have her get the girls when they get out of school and take them to their grandmother. Kelly, pack what you need to be away two days—for all of you. And decide where you're going. House will be off limits."

I was stunned. All I wanted was to go back to bed and hide forever, and he was telling me to pack my family for two days? I couldn't believe it.

Conroy gentled a bit. "Kelly, I'm sorry. I understand how you feel. To shoot somebody kills a little bit of your soul, and you'll probably never be quite the same person again. It makes you see life and death differently. But I can't step in the way of police procedure." He turned to Mike, "Shandy, find that damn walker and help this woman."

Mike said grimly, "I can do it without the walker." First he called Keisha, who said, "I knew she shouldn't stay home. I was on my way over there. Got to listen to myself better."

I grabbed the phone. "Keisha, don't tell the girls I shot two people. God! I couldn't bear for them to know that. Just tell them there was a problem at the house. Tell them Bella won't be following us anymore. Take them for ice cream. Do whatever. Please?"

"You got it," she said, "What do I need to do for you? I'm kickin' myself over here. I should have come babysat you. Wouldn't have been no gunfire."

Mike grabbed the phone. "It's too late for 'what if,' Keisha. Call Nana and Claire and Anthony, please. But tell them no visitors. We don't even know where we'll be."

"You'll be at Miss Cynthia's house. Ain't no choice about that."

She was right. The four of us moved in with Mom. She would have it no other way. Mike and I took the guest room bed, and the girls both slept with Mom. Keisha brought the girls, who were puzzled and upset even without knowing that their mother had shot two people.

"Why can't I go home?" Maggie wailed. "My pajamas are there."

"I brought your pajamas," I said. "We're all going to have a sleepover at Nana's."

Em didn't brighten much at the prospect.

"Something bad happened, Maggie," Em replied calmly, "and they don't want us to know about it."

Mike and I exchanged looks and realized we had to tell the girls the truth. If they thought we were hiding something, they'd never trust us again. So we all sat down, and I told them my story. "This morning, after I took you to school and Mike to the substation, I went back home to take a nap. While I was sort of half asleep, Bella and her brother, Ben, broke into our house. They meant to harm me, and I...I shot them."

Maggie gasped and hugged me tight, but Em asked, "Are they dead?" Her little voice was so calm and the look on her face so...oh, I don't know...inquisitive, unemotional. She was almost clinical. It made me bury my face in my hands.

"No, Em, they're both in the hospital. They're going to be all right, but they're going to jail for a long time."

"We don't have to worry about that green car following us?" Maggie asked.

"No, no green car." Some deep instinct made me add,

"But we still have to be afraid." After all, Tom Lattimore hadn't called. Maybe instead of worrying about him, I should be worrying about his plans for me and my family. Maybe the two goons who beat Otto up would take over where Bella and Ben had failed. The possibilities for danger were endless.

Keisha appointed herself phone monitor. Everyone in the world called—Claire wanted us to come to her house because it was larger, Anthony wanted to come see for himself that I was alright—I nearly told him I would never be alright again. Joe melted my heart when he said, "Tell Miss Kelly, when she feels better, not even to think about going to the Garzas' house. I'll go up there before I go to work tomorrow. I know the things to say to her. She knows about her kids, and I'll make her accept it." Joe knew that a visit to Mrs. Garza would be on my mind. Keisha did allow one visitor—Claire, who brought dinner and wine for all of us. Mom was too upset to cook.

We ate roast beef and mashed potatoes and salad on disposable plates, drank wine out of plastic cups, and threw the whole thing in the trash. No cleanup. Claire left, saying, "Call me in the morning. The world will look better to you."

We urged Keisha to go home and get some sleep. We'd be safe with Mike there and José patrolling. She insisted she wasn't budging. "It ain't over yet. I'm the fat lady, and I haven't sung yet. I'm sleeping on the couch."

Mike knew better than to protest.

I pestered Mike every half hour to call JPS and check on the condition of the Garzas. Ben had been rushed into surgery, but Conroy was right. I hadn't hit any vital organs, though the bullet had nicked his intestine and they took out his appendix while they were in there. He'd have the usual slow recovery from abdominal surgery, but he'd live to stand trial.

"Trial?"

"For breaking and entering, attempted murder. Conroy will probably drum up some other charges. Ben's a juvenile but not for long. He'll end up in Huntsville or some similar facility. Bella will face the same charges and will go to prison. They're out of our lives, Kelly."

"But why? Who? What?" I sounded like advice given to a rookie newspaper reporter, but there was too much missing from this story. There was someone bigger behind this, someone who paid Ben and Bella to stalk me and probably to kill me. Tom Lattimore must hold the clue, I thought. "Mike, Tom Lattimore never called me back."

He shrugged. "Kelly, I was worried about him. But right now my concern is my family. Tom Lattimore can damn well fend for himself."

I literally fell into bed about eight, leaving Mom to get the girls to bed and Mike to help himself. I thought I'd sleep for a lifetime.

Mike's phone rang in the night. When he answered it with "Shandy," I felt a cold chill shoot through my body. He mumbled a few things like, "Okay," "Yeah, we'll talk tomorrow." Nothing that revealed what was going on.

I roused enough to ask, "Mike? What?"

"Nothing, Kelly. Go back to sleep. You need it."

"No," I said stubbornly. "Tell me what's happened."

Mike knew the tone of voice. "They found Lattimore's body in an alley on the North Side. Stabbed."

"Bella! But no, she couldn't have done it. She was at our house trying to kill me." I thought the words would send me into a paroxysm of giggling—someone had actually set out to kill me. Unbelievable. "The goons who beat up Otto." I knew instinctively that was the answer. *Why had I forgotten about those two thugs?*

"Possibly. You'll have to wait for the ME to announce the time of death, as close as possible, to rule out Bella and

Ben. Don't go jumping to conclusions."

"It's all mixed up together," I said, "but we still don't know why. There's somebody out there, somebody who still wants me dead." I shivered and cuddled closer to the protective arm he put around me. "Mike, no big-box store on Magnolia is that important. What's going on?"

He stroked my hair and murmured, "Kelly, I don't know. But we won't solve it tonight. Go back to sleep."

Of course I didn't. I lay awake all night.

Chapter Nineteen

Keisha was fixing breakfast while I sat with coffee and stared into space. When my cell phone rang, caller I.D. said John Henry Jackson. What could he want two days before Christmas? "Kelly O'Connell," I said sort of abruptly.

"Little lady, I am so glad you're all right. I read about the attack on you in the newspaper this morning."

Well, darn. There was publicity I didn't need. Who trusts a real estate agent who keeps getting involved in crimes? Keisha was eyeing me sternly, but I blithely ignored her. I thanked John Henry for his concern, assured him I was all right, just scared, and that we were at my mom's until the police cleared the crime scene tape.

After I hung up, Keisha demanded, "Can't you ever just say thank you, Merry Christmas and goodbye? Why you tellin' him where we are?"

I was too tired to argue. "John Henry's just concerned. He's a marshmallow. He called me 'little lady' again."

"Today, I don't trust nobody."

"Wish Mom took the newspaper so I could see the article John Henry mentioned. I'll go ask Mike to pull it up on the computer."

Finally I got a laugh from Keisha. "Your mom don't take the newspaper 'cause she says this still isn't her city and she don't know the people it talks about."

"Oh, for Pete's sake."

"Get everybody in here for breakfast while you're at it. These eggs gonna get cold."

Mike pulled up the paper and we found a brief mention in the local news note section. It didn't have much beside what John Henry had told me. Said there been a break-and-enter incident at a residence and then gave our specific address: street and house number. An open invitation to other no-gooders. Mike muttered, "Damn!"

We mostly stared at each other all morning. My mind was on the thousand things I had to do to get ready for Christmas, but oddly I couldn't focus on any one. Claire called to announce she had worked out a potluck assignment, so everyone else was bringing dinner to my house on Christmas Day. I wasn't to cook a thing. I'd have my hands full just wrapping Christmas presents, and I guessed we'd have a tree trimming party whenever. Before New Year's for sure.

About noon Conroy knocked on the door. When Keisha opened it, he said, "Boy, do I have news." He was more animated than I'd ever seen him and couldn't bring himself to sit still. He paced, while he told us the morning's discoveries.

The homicide guys had searched Lattimore's apartment first thing in the morning. It had already been tossed, during the night, by someone looking for something specific. Pillows and sofa cushions were torn open, pictures yanked off the wall and their backings ripped, the computer gone but the flat-screen television and a bunch of cash was left behind. They even theorized that Tom might have been surprised in his apartment and kidnapped. But they found something important that had been overlooked: a safe deposit box key. Opening it required a warrant to force the bank to let them open it, and they had to work fast, since banks would close early because of the approaching holiday. By ten, they were at the bank, warrant and key in hand, and opened the box.

"Damndest thing," Conroy said. "I think your pal," he directed that at me, "knew he wasn't long for this world. He printed out a whole confession—implicated...oh, you'll never guess. John Henry Jackson, our history-minded lawyer, *was* North Side Properties and also was the brains behind this whole grocery store, which was a front for growing and shipping marijuana. Get it? Wild Things? That temperature-controlled shed was really a growing room. His investors? Non-existent. He wasn't sharing this cash cow with anyone. He wanted that specific location because of its easy access to trucking routes. Besides, putting an upscale grocery in your neighborhood was a good cover."

John Henry! My mind refused to grasp that idea. He hadn't just called to be nice. He wanted to know what I knew—and I told him enough. I confessed to Conroy, who waved my concern away. "John Henry probably already had the computer in his possession and had read the confession. He's probably on his way out of town. We've got an APB out on him and have notified airports, railroad counters, even the bus depot. We'll get him."

I felt all the air go out of me as I sank into the couch, deflated, angry, confused. No wonder the landmark commission had approved the project—I wondered if they'd even seen it or John Henry had just rubber-stamped it. Such duplicity was beyond me. And what about Robert Lawler? Did he even know his name was used to give respectability to a fictional list of investors? I doubted it.

Mike and Conroy talked quietly in a corner and then Mike came over to shake my shoulder, jarring me out of my reverie and back into the present.

"He says we can get back in the house this afternoon. I'll feel better to be on the premises." He thought for a minute. "Let's leave the girls here. At least until I feel sure the house is safe."

Keisha approved our plan. "It's a pretty day. I'll take the girls—and Miss Cynthia if she wants to go—to the zoo. If that's okay."

Mom declined. "Whoever heard of going to the zoo

two days before Christmas? I have too much to do. Besides, it's December!"

"Mom, it's going to be seventy today, a perfect day for the zoo." I turned to Mike. "You think they'll be safe?"

"With Keisha, of course. As Buck said, Jackson is probably trying desperately to get out of town. Hurting you—or us—won't do him any good now."

"Maybe José will drag himself out of bed," she said. "I'll go call him. He's off tonight, has to work Christmas." She made a face.

It all worked out. José came to Mom's and the four of them set off, with plans for dinner at the Grill after the zoo trip. I drove Mike and me to the house, and Mom set about baking Christmas pies—pumpkin and pecan.

It was strange to go back in the house. Everything was orderly. The window had been replaced, furniture straightened, blood removed from the doorways, hall carpet torn up exposing lovely hardwood floors that I would not re-carpet. The Christmas tree was still in place, undecorated—we had planned to have our own tree-trimming party last night But still it felt...funny.

"Mike, does it smell different?"

He sniffed. "No. What do you think you smell?"

"Uh, dried blood?"

"That's your imagination. Get busy and you'll forget about it. Wrap Christmas presents. Make a grocery list. Do all that stuff you were going to do yesterday. I'm going to check out the guest apartment. I'll use the ramp in front."

At the door, he hesitated, threw me a look of defiance, and shoved his walker aside, picking up the cane the doctor had recently okayed for his use. I went back to the bedroom to dig presents out of the closet—having the girls gone for the day was a blessing.

I had wrapped two packages—clothes for the girls— when Mike called from the living room, "Kelly, can you come here?" His voice was so tight it grated on my nerves. Something made me wish for my pistol, but the police still had it. And Mike probably was carrying his.

"Kelly, now!"

Defenseless, I walked down the hall and found John Henry holding a gun to Mike's back.

"He was hiding in the apartment," Mike said tightly. "I've told him there's nothing to be gained now, but he wants to use us as hostages to negotiate a clean get-away."

"Not both of you, just the little lady." He turned to me, his gun still trained on Mike. "I tried to keep you out of this. But you wouldn't listen to me, to Bella, probably even to your obliging husband here. Now you're my ticket to Mexico. You're going with me. If all goes well, I'll put you on a plane back to DFW. If not...," he shrugged. "I'll do whatever I have to. I'm not going to jail."

Appalled, scared, you name it. "You can't be serious!" I could feel the blood rush to my face and my knees went weak again. Damn! I'd been feeling this way too often in the past couple of days. John Henry, the man I dismissed as a marshmallow, was threatening something unfathomable. Mexico? I couldn't. I wouldn't. He pointed the gun at me.

"I assure you, I'm deadly serious...and that's not a play on words." His usually laughing eyes had gone steel-cold blue, and he alternated his gaze between intimidating me— it worked!—and keeping an eye on Mike.

I was desperately searching every corner of my mind for a way out of this.

"Move," John barked, holding the gun steadily in my direction. He knew Mike wouldn't move if I was in danger. "Plane is not pressurized...grab a coat. That's all, and I'm watching."

As I turned to the closet, out of the corner of my eye I caught a flicker of movement on the porch. I dared not react with a sigh of relief or a glance. Thank heaven the curtains were sheer—whoever was out there could look in and see the scene we were in the middle of. Stalling for time seemed my best option.

"I need time…tell my girls…take some things with me. A toothbrush."

"No time. I'll buy whatever you need when we reach our destination. Come now. We're through stalling."

The first coat I grabbed out of the closet was Mike's ski jacket—no chance he'd left a gun in the pocket. John Henry's gun was still pointed at me, and he said, in a jokingly gallant tone, "After you, my dear. I'll be right behind you. Go out the front door. You may say goodbye to your husband from a distance."

I turned to Mike and saw he had turned to me. Our eyes locked, but John Henry couldn't decipher the message we sent each other—and the prayer for safety for both of us. Who knew what would happen once I went out that door?

John Henry spoke to Mike over his shoulder, keeping the gun trained on me. "If you value your wife, wait one hour before calling your comrades. We're taking her car. You'll find it eventually." Then, to me, "Open the door, little lady."

I opened the door with apprehension, wondering who was outside. The thought came too late that it could be an accomplice of John Henry. But when I took that first step beyond the door, I realized that a sudden norther had hit. My first thought was that the girls would be cold at the zoo. Before I could worry about that, there was a commotion behind me.

I stood stock still, expecting a bullet in the back. Instead, I felt a sharp stinging pain in my left calf and then wetness. Then I heard Keisha shouting, "Oh my god, you hit Kelly!" Far from being scared or worried about a wound, I wanted to laugh out loud.

Behind me, John Henry lay on the porch, clutching his right wrist, and José stood over him with a gun. Mike was in the doorway and on the phone. Keisha was on her knees, pulling up my pants leg and shouting, "José, go get some paper towels."

"I can't," he replied calmly. "I'm holding the gun on our friend here."

She dashed off toward the kitchen and returned quickly with paper towels, wet and dry. As Keisha began, sponging at my leg, which now really stung, José explained.

"Keisha got one of her feelings."

Keisha looked up at me. "I just knew you were in trouble. I told José we had to hotfoot it to your house, but we did drop the girls off with Miss Cynthia first. Looks like we just made it."

Stunned. Irrelevant thought: *The girls aren't freezing at the zoo.* "What happened?" I pointed to John Henry who lay motionless and refusing to speak.

José nudged him with a boot. "I karate chopped his gun hand as he came out the door. Think I broke his wrist—least that's what I wanted to do. Didn't give him time to shoot, but his gun went off and the bullet grazed your leg. Sorry, but it's better than the alternative."

"Definitely," I agreed, putting most of my weight on my right leg. Keisha had straightened up and announced I needed to go to an emergency clinic or doc-in-a-box or something.

"Not until Conroy gets here," Mike said, "Kelly, you okay?"

I nodded. It hurt, but not that badly.

"I told you not to trust anybody, even when they talk nice," Keisha said righteously.

"John Henry, what do you have to say?" I demanded. "Mexico, indeed."

"You probably wouldn't have ever come back," he

said, and that sent chills down my spine.

Of course, Conroy led the charge, but it looked like the entire homicide squad arrived to take John Henry downtown. Now he refused to say anything except, "I want a lawyer."

"You are a lawyer," Conroy said viciously, "not that it's going to do you much good."

The whole story came out slowly, thanks to Tom's lengthy confession—now I almost felt sorry for him—and the few things John Henry said, after he got a lawyer. He denied killing either Sonny Adams or Tom Lattimore, and Conroy said he'd face charges of conspiracy to murder.

"Harder for the prosecution to build its case, but they can do it. They found Lattimore's computer in John Henry's plane."

Thinking of the plane ride I almost took, I asked, "Where was it?"

"Private air strip south of town. Owner said he knew John Henry professionally, didn't think anything of his request to park the plane there a few days ago and then today he got notice that Jackson'd be taking off. He figured John Henry would file a flight plan and play it according to the rules. We're checkin' it out but I think he's in the clear. Sweating a bit, though. Said he always thought John Henry was most law abiding."

"So did we all," I said.

Epilogue

We never did find out where in Mexico John Henry planned to go, and I didn't even want to think about it.

Keisha sent José off with Conroy, who would have demanded he come along to recount his version of the story, even if Keisha hadn't insisted. Then she took Mike and me to the emergency room at JPS since she declared neither of us could drive. A strip mall clinic would have done just fine, but we figured the personnel at the county hospital knew Mike and we'd get in and out.

We did. The graze on my leg was sterilized and dressed, and I was given supplies for dressing it at home.

"We've got to go to the girls. They'll be scared to death, and so will Mom."

So we went to Mom's house, where indeed we were greeted by two wailing girls and a mom who was wringing her hands in despair. I assured them I was all right, Mike was all right, and it hadn't been a big deal.

"Well, I declare, if it wasn't a big deal, Keisha don't you ever scare me like that again. Dropping off these girls as if the devil himself was chasing you!"

"Yes, ma'am, Miss Cynthia. I'm sorry for having worried you." Keisha could play quiet and contrite every bit as well as she did bold and brassy.

The girls hovered over me, examined my leg, and asked how I hurt it. Since I vowed never to lie to them, I said, "A bullet grazed it."

"God in Heaven," Mom cried, raising her arms to the heavens above. "What has my child gotten herself into?" She glared at Mike, as though blaming him for involving me in police matters.

He spread his hands in that age-old "I don't know" gesture and said, "Don't blame me, Nana. She gets herself into these things. I was almost a victim of her foolishness this time." But he kissed the top of my head and hugged me.

We were a tired bunch. Keisha took the four of us home and went on to wait for José at their apartment. "I guess I can move out of the guest house," she said. "I'll do it tomorrow."

Mike fried some sausage, fixed scrambled eggs, and we all fell into bed right after we ate. The girls brought pallets and slept on the floor next to our bed. I figured they needed reassurance this night.

Of course, I dreamt about flying to Mexico with John Henry at the controls of a small plane—frightening image! But I'd waken myself and reach out for Mike, and I knew all was well.

****

We gathered for Christmas dinner at Claire's. She insisted, after the trauma with John Henry. Mike, the girls, and I opened gifts at home around an undecorated tree, and some of the gifts were not wrapped. But it was a joyous Christmas morning. Mike fixed poached eggs on toast and cheese, a concoction he called Huck Finns. He had to explain to the girls about Huck Finn and the raft down the Mississippi River, but they still looked puzzled.

At Claire's house, everyone wanted to know the blow-by-blow details of our encounter with John Henry, and we obliged. They deserved to know, since they put up with all my antics and cheered me on. José and Keisha came in to loud cheering for their part in the adventure. Mom remained aloof from the telling and tried to frown in disapproval but Otto sat by her and commented frequently, sometimes turning to Mom to say, "You must be so proud of her. She saved my store."

What could Mom do except smile and agree?

Anthony and Joe muttered about what they'd do if they got their hands on John Henry, and Keisha scoffed at them. "You men need to wait for my sixth sense to tell you what to do."

José just grinned.

We ate—and ate—turkey and dressing and mashed potatoes, with gravy over all, and green beans and sweet potatoes and cranberry and pecan and chocolate meringue pies until we groaned. Toasts were made to health, wealth, and happiness.

Mike proposed a toast to a life without adventures and even my girls joined in shouting, "Hear, hear!"

I sat in the glow of fellowship and thought surely our lives would be peaceful from now on.

THE END

ABOUT JUDY ALTER

Judy Alter is the author of the Kelly O'Connell Mysteries, *Skeleton in a Dead Space, No Neighborhood for Old Women,* and the new *Trouble in a Big Box.* An award-winning novelist, she has written fiction for adults and young adults, primarily about women of the American West, and turned her attention to cozy mysteries in the last few years with admirable success.

Look for future books from Judy Alter

Ghost in a Four-Square
and
Murder at the Blue Plate Café

If you enjoyed Judy Alter's *Trouble in a Big Box*,
you might also enjoy these authors
published by Turquoise Morning Press:

Maddie James, author of *Murder on the Mountain*
Bobbye Terry, author of *Buried in Briny Bay*
Christina Wolfer, author of *The Daughter*

Thank you!

for purchasing this book from
Turquoise Morning Press.

We invite you to visit our Web site to learn more about our
quality Trade Paperback and eBook selections.

As a gift to you for purchasing this book, please use
COUPON CODE Ebook15 during your visit to receive
15% off any digital title in our Turquoise Morning Press
Bookstore.

www.turquoisemorningpressbookstore.com

Turquoise Morning Press
Because every good beach deserves a book.
www.turquoisemorningpress.com
~~~~

15736406R00134

Made in the USA
Charleston, SC
17 November 2012